I've been living with this movie for more than four years, and people have often come to me and said, "How can you work on one project for so long?" It's the constant awe and the constant inspiration from the work of other people that keep me going. One of the great things about animation, and especially what we do with computer animation, is that every step of the way you see something new.

Making the first computer animated feature film has been an exciting process. On the one hand we knew that we were creating something that no one has ever seen before. But on the other hand we had to respect the fact that the story and the characters had to be absolutely great or people weren't going to sit in their theater seats and watch all this brand-new imagery.

I have found that part of my job is to educate, inform, and inspire the people working on the film, but more often than not, I am the one who is informed, educated, and inspired by everybody else's work.

There is so much joy in the process for me. I feel lucky to be able to come to work every day and see parts of the movie and say, "Oh wow! Look at that. That's amazing."

—JOHN LASSETER, Director

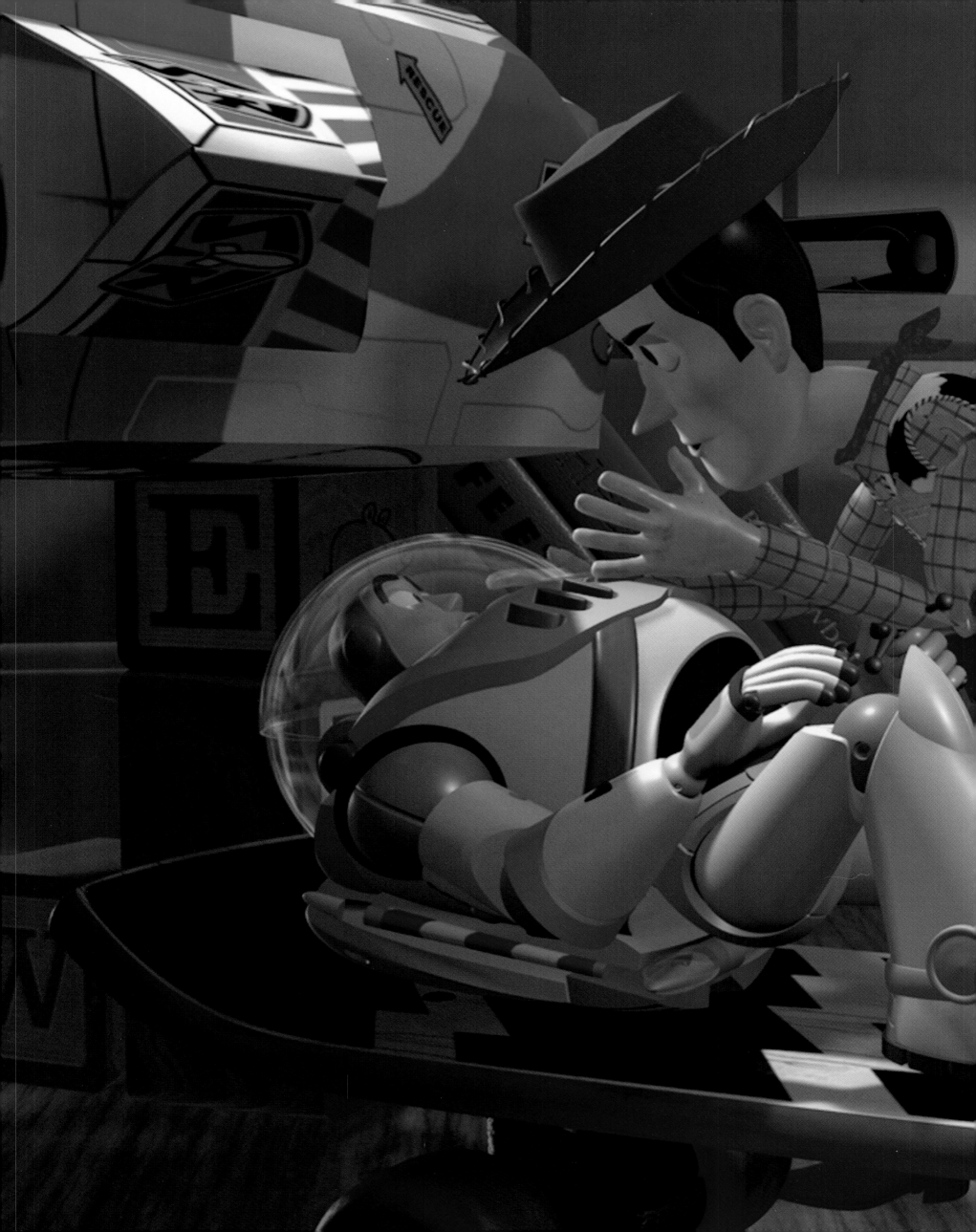

TOY STORY

The Art and Making of the Animated Film

Text by
John Lasseter and Steve Daly

A WELCOME BOOK

HYPERION

NEW YORK

ACKNOWLEDGMENTS

The producers and authors of *Toy Story: The Art and Making of the Animated Film* wish to thank the following people for their extraordinary contributions to the creation of this book: Bonnie Arnold, Edwin Catmull, Monica Corbin, Deirdre Cossman, Pete Docter, Ralph Eggleston, Stacie Fenster, Howard Green, Ralph Guggenheim, Alethea Harampolis, Stacie Iverson, Andy King, Fumi Kitahara, Zoë Leader, Robert Lence, Tim Lewis, Joe Ranft, Bill Reeves, Peter Schneider, Russell Schroeder, Thomas Schumacher, Andrew Stanton, Deirdre Warin, and Joss Whedon. We would additionally like to thank every artist, technician, and administrator at Pixar and at Disney who shared their time, their commitment, and their stories.

For information address
HYPERION
114 Fifth Avenue, New York, NY 10011

Produced by
WELCOME ENTERPRISES, INC.
575 Broadway, New York, NY 10012

Project Director: HIRO CLARK
Editor: ELLEN MENDLOW
Hyperion Editor: WENDY LEFKON
Designer: GREGORY WAKABAYASHI

Library of Congress Cataloging-in-Publication Data
Lasseter, John.
Toy story : the art and making of the animated film /
text by John Lasseter and Steve Daly.
p.   cm.
ISBN 0-7868-6180-0
1. Animated films.   I. Daly, Steve, 1962– .   II. Title.
NC1765.L35 1995
791.43'72—dc20   95-32296
CIP

FIRST EDITION
Printed and bound in Singapore by Toppan Printing Co., Inc.
1 3 5 7 9 10 8 6 4 2

CONTENTS

To Infinity and Beyond

6

A Created World

14

A Great Story and Great Characters

26

A Visual Feast

51

An Emotional Journey

92

To Infinity and Beyond

"Two companies came together—one massive and experienced, the other small, scrappy, and brilliant—each bringing extraordinary resources to the table."

—THOMAS SCHUMACHER, Senior Vice President, Walt Disney Feature Animation

CONCEPT ART BY STEVE JOHNSON.

CONCEPT ART BY JEFF PIDGEON.

In the early 1990s, when the use of computer animation in motion pictures was only just beginning to garner public attention, director John Lasseter and his colleagues at Pixar were working on a story idea that could play as a feature-length film to be created entirely with computer-generated imagery. Having already achieved enormous success with award-winning computer animated shorts and commercials, they felt the time had come to move on toward a long cherished goal. "We were aiming to make a feature right from the beginning," says Pixar president Edwin Catmull, who along with Lasseter, producer Ralph Guggenheim, supervising technical director Bill Reeves, and their team of graphics experts left Lucasfilm and, together with Steve Jobs, formed Pixar in 1986.

Around the same time Pixar began pursuing its dream in earnest, Walt Disney Feature Animation had started to expand into forms of animation beyond the traditional two-dimensional cel process it had already perfected. The first step was a partnership with Tim Burton to create *Nightmare Before Christmas* using the stop-motion process.

"It'll be a buddy movie: a banter–laden tale of a bitter alliance blossoming into a true friendship. It'll have a few unusual twists. First, the buddies will be toys. And second, it will be the first time an entire movie will have been created using computer animation."

—JOHN LASSETER, Director

With *Beauty and the Beast*, Disney successfully employed computer animation in creating the backgrounds and some animation for several scenes. As a next step, Feature Animation began to contemplate doing what no one else had done before— creating the world's first full-length computer animated film.

Enter Pixar.

"John Lasseter was a natural for us," recalls Peter Schneider, president of Walt Disney Feature Animation. "He made short films in the computer animated format and he did it better than anybody else in the world." In 1986, Pixar had garnered the first-ever Academy Award® nomination for a 3-D computer animated short with *Luxo Jr.*, which it followed two years later with *Tin Toy*, the first computer animated short to win an Academy Award®. "Pixar knows how to create a scene on the computer screen using computer technology better than anyone else in the universe," adds Feature Animation senior vice president Thomas Schumacher. "They do it brilliantly and beautifully and with much more warmth and appeal than anyone else working in this

Above: BUZZ CONCEPT ART BY NILO RODIS.
Top: WOODY CONCEPT ART BY BUD LUCKEY.

CONCEPT ART BY TIA KRATTER.

"The artists and technicians at Feature Animation bring to the table a fundamental belief that anything can be done. It's just a matter of putting the right people together to get it done."

—PETER SCHNEIDER, President, Walt Disney Feature Animation

Above: CONCEPT ART BY DAVE GORDON.
Top: SLINKY CONCEPT ART BY BUD LUCKEY.
Below: CONCEPT ART BY ANDREW STANTON.

medium. John Lasseter loves a created world, so what a great place for his work, this technology. But the work you see really comes from John's heart and his spirit, as much as it comes out of a computer box. And that is the big thing that separates Pixar from every other computer animation company."

In fact, John Lasseter was no stranger to Disney, having been an animator for the studio at one time before heading north to San Francisco and the world of computer technology. Additionally, Pixar had already established a relationship with the Studio. In 1988, it was part of the development of the CAPS system for Disney, an electronic ink-and-paint technology that would receive an Academy Award® for technical merit. "We had wanted to do a movie with John for a long time," recalls Schneider, adding, "we tried to hire him back to work at Disney."

Lasseter, however, preferred to remain at Pixar, and consequently, when the decision was made to pursue their common dream, a partnership was created that in a practical sense allowed each side to draw on the other's strengths and talents to develop a story and devise a production system that would carry the film through an arduous creative process. What Disney brought to the table was its considerable experience in feature-length filmmaking. "We know how to actually get this stuff put together in seventy-five minutes of film," says Schumacher. "We know how to track a movie, make a movie, look at it, edit it, cut sound effects, cut music, and review it. These are things that Pixar had never done. In many ways they didn't know what they didn't know because no one had ever done this before."

Indeed, one of the earliest and most difficult tasks required Pixar to hire the

"If short films are sprints, features are marathons, especially in animation. You're talking about a four-year commitment."

—BONNIE ARNOLD, Producer

Above: CONCEPT ART BY TIA KRATTER.
Top left: SID CONCEPT ART BY STEVE JOHNSON.
Top right: ANDY CONCEPT DRAWING BY BUD LUCKEY.

Above: A PANEL FROM THE PASTEL COLOR SCRIPT BY RALPH EGGLESTON.
Right: CONCEPT ART BY BUD LUCKEY.

"Nobody knew what skills we'd need when we started. It was a completely new series of combinations that had to add up to more than the sum of its parts."

—RALPH GUGGENHEIM, Producer

STORYBOARD ART BY ANDREW STANTON.

animation, editing, and post-production staff that would create the film. To help with the management of this process Bonnie Arnold, who comes from a live-action movie background (associate producer, *Dances With Wolves*), joined Ralph Guggenheim as a producer about a year into production. Together they worked to design systems and budgets that would keep the studio functioning at top productivity. "No one had ever done this type of movie before," says Guggenheim. "How do you design the process? How do you design the studio? How do you find the people? How do you pull together all these people into a cohesive unit?" Adds Arnold, "We didn't really know what our path was and what we were trying to do was keep this growing monster on that unknown path." Kathleen Gavin, vice president of production for special projects at Walt Disney Feature Animation, tried to smooth the way a bit. Having co-produced *Nightmare Before Christmas*, Gavin brought a wealth of experience in finding potential problems in an unfamiliar medium. "Part of my role," she says, "was to help Pixar identify big black holes they might be headed for."

The process of developing the story, from the initial pitch to a workable script, was led by Lasseter, Schneider, Schumacher, story co-creator Andrew Stanton, supervising animator Pete Docter, and story co-creator Joe Ranft, a veteran of many Disney productions. The screenplay was developed by Joss Whedon (*Buffy the Vampire*

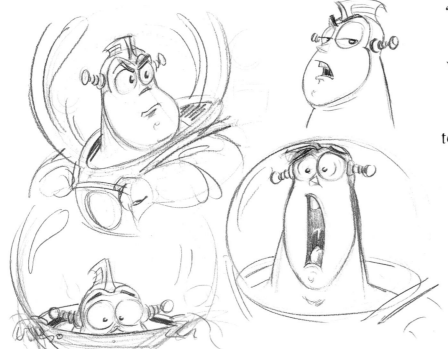

Above: CONCEPT ART BY WILLIAM JOYCE.
Left: BUZZ CONCEPT ART BY BUD LUCKEY.

Slayer), Andrew Stanton, Joel Cohen, and Alec Sokolow. Composer Randy Newman (*Avalon*, *The Natural*, *Ragtime*), working closely with Disney's executive music producer Chris Montan, was brought aboard to compose a unique score and songs that would help maintain the film's high emotional pitch. The responsibility for executing the action with an emphasis on believability and for realizing the film's detail-filled environment came under the painstaking care of art director Ralph Eggleston and Bill Reeves.

Through all the hard work that went into making *Toy Story*, it became clear that what Pixar and Disney created was a remarkable collaboration that would take them on a journey that neither could have completely imagined when they first set out. "I think there's a certain degree of magic that occurred in Pixar and Disney coming together to make this film," says Guggenheim. "Each group stretched beyond what they would normally do to create something new and different." Adds Schneider, "At Disney we have the belief that every time we do something it is unique. And the Pixar group shares that fundamental belief that they are doing what no one's ever done before."

Or as John Lasseter put it, "I felt a lot like Buzz Lightyear popping out of that cardboard box into the great unknown."

Above: CONCEPT ART BY DAVE GORDON.
Overleaf: CONCEPT ART BY TIA KRATTER.

A CREATED WORLD

"To me there's no object that can't
become a personality."

—JOHN LASSETER

What's the most distinguishing feature of any real-life kid's room? The helter-skelter mix of toys. Big toys, little toys, tough action figures, cute little preschool block people are all piled together shoulder to shoulder, even though they conjure up markedly different moods, scales, and kinds of play. Out of that observation came *Toy Story*'s inspired central conceit: What if all these unique playthings had one thing in common—they came to life the moment humans weren't around?

Above: BO PEEP CONCEPT ART BY BUD LUCKEY.
Top: STORYBOARD ART BY JOE RANFT.
Right: CONCEPT ART OF ANDY'S ROOM
BY BUD LUCKEY.

"The quality of the acting in *Toy Story* makes you believe the toys are real. But people have a predisposition to begin with to believe in their toys. All we're doing is saying your fantasies are right."

—PETER SCHNEIDER

ROCKY GIBRALTAR CONCEPT ART
BY BUD LUCKEY.

"This bedroom is a little urban microcosm. It's a melting pot that isn't so melted. It's got toys of different plastics and colors and sizes and recommended age groups all doing their jobs together and living on top of one another. So they can get a little testy."

—JOHN LASSETER

The task of bringing the *Toy Story* cast to life began with thinking through each toy's physical and conceptual essence. How is it made? What was it built to do? What are its physical flaws and limitations? Out of this exploration came a cast of characters as diverse as the materials from which they were made. The key to defining each of the toys' personalities, says Lasseter, was to try always to derive their traits from the realities of their construction, respecting what he calls the "physical integrity of the object." Mr. Potato Head (voiced by Don Rickles) is a natural malcontent. Explains Lasseter, "You'd have a chip on your shoulder too if your face kept falling off all day." By the same extrapolative thinking, porcelain Bo Peep (Annie Potts) becomes a delicate flirt: She has to move carefully, or she'll break. Cheap-plastic Rex (Wallace Shawn) doesn't thunder around like a living tyrannosaur from *Jurassic Park*; he's stiff and tentative and unsure of himself because his construction makes him limited in what he can do. Hamm the piggy bank

STORYBOARD ART BY JEFF PIDGEON.

(John Ratzenberger) sits on a shelf all day above the other toys and thinks he's a pretty superior fellow, always sure his two cents matter. And wobbly, slow-footed Slinky (Jim Varney) can't move under his own power nearly as easily as when he's pulled along, so he's happy to follow Woody, the leader.

Binding all the toys in a somewhat contentious sense of community is their common purpose in life: to be played with. "Every man-made object is manufactured for a reason, and their reason for being is to make children happy," says Lasseter. "Anything that interferes with that is unsettling to them."

"We were lucky enough that if there's one thing animators know, it's their childhood and their toys. We're all just grown-up kids."

—ANDREW STANTON, Story Co-creator

"My number one goal is believability. As a moviegoer, I'm always thinking to myself, do I buy that a character would do this? Do I believe the story would take this turn?"

—JOHN LASSETER

As Lasseter and the *Toy Story* crew set off to make this first-ever computer animated film, believability was arguably the most important overarching principle. The creators reached not for mere verisimilitude, not for an exact duplicate of mundane reality, but for a created world in which the design of the characters and environment provides an enhanced, hyper-real version of real life.

"The tactileness of this world, even though it never has existed—the sense that you can reach out and hold what you see on the screen—is very significant to the appeal of the film. If you tried to make it look like real life, you would fail, because it will never look like real life, but it can be touchable life."

—THOMAS SCHUMACHER

Above: CONCEPT ART BY TIA KRATTER.
Top: CONCEPT ART BY BUD LUCKEY.

"Little green army men can't suddenly move in a way that a kid playing with them wouldn't picture them moving. They can't just act like human soldiers. When they're alive, they still have to move like toy soldiers."

—JOHN LASSETER

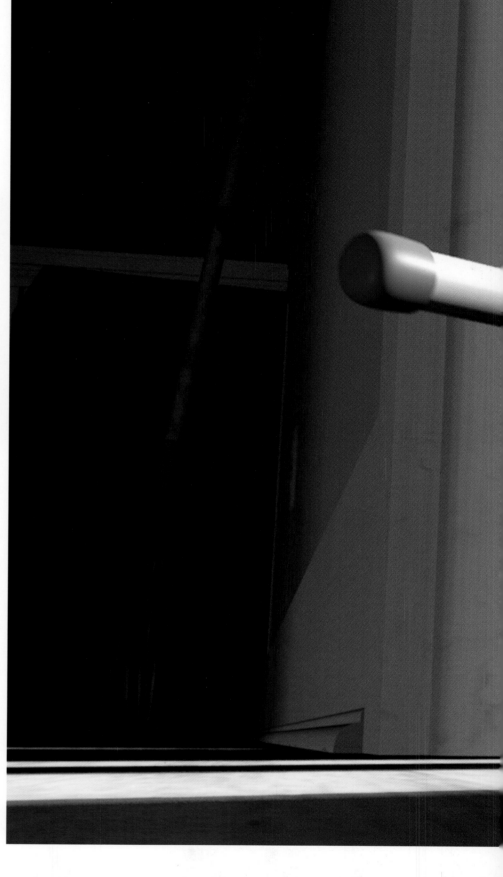

"With this movie we were finally telling a story where we could execute stuff that we've always wished we could see our toys do. That was the motivating emotion that got us into it. That desire to believe in your toys."

—ANDREW STANTON

The little green army men who stage a reconnaissance mission at Andy's birthday party are a clear example of the principles at work in creating *Toy Story*'s believable world. "Practically every American male had little green army men as a kid," says John Lasseter. "The one standing with the mine sweeper, the one on his knee with the bazooka, all of that. We had to be true to that burned-in memory." At the command of R. Lee Ermey, the real-life drill instructor from Stanley Kubrick's *Full Metal Jacket*, who supplied the lead sergeant's voice, the soldiers hop on legs permanently stuck to crude plastic bases. And despite their pathetically poor tools, they are professionals who take their jobs very, very seriously.

For the animators, getting these soldiers to "Move! Move! Move!" with just the right erratic, evocative gait required special weapons and tactics. Pete Docter nailed a pair of old running

THE RECONNAISSANCE TEAM OF GREEN ARMY MEN STRIKE THEIR ORIGINAL POSES AS ANDY'S MOM APPROACHES.

THE THREE ICONIC TRAITS OF GREEN ARMY MEN: BENT
GUN BARRELS, EXCESS PLASTIC—OR MOLD FLASHES—
AND FEET IRREVOCABLY ATTACHED TO TINY OVOID BASES.

shoes to a big board, and his dedicated corps of artists took turns hobbling around the hallways, studying each other's awkward steps. "We tried lots of different pogo-stick jumps, different swings," recalls Docter. "That gave us some ideas about where your energy goes when you can't move your feet, and how your hips would move relative to a base if, um, you had one." Meticulous care, too, went into analyzing how plastic parachutes would open from the great height of a second-floor landing, and exactly how the pint-sized soldiers would sway in suburban hallway air currents while suspended from those clunky rings on their helmets. As it turned out, none of the animators could actually replicate the hippety-hop locomotion they finally engineered for their characters. But as Docter says, "That's why you animate something. You can give it moves you'd never see in the real world."

> "We want people to believe that these toy and human characters live in this world we've created—ride in these cars, sleep in these beds, walk in these hallways. Achieving that is the starting point for engaging the audience."
>
> —JOHN LASSETER

The members of the art department, led by Ralph Eggleston, visual designers Bob Pauley and Bill Cone, and digital painters Tia Kratter and Robin Cooper, were responsible for the degree of detail and sense of reality on every visual level from the largest set to the lighting to the smallest props. From scuff marks on baseboards and wear marks on the floor, to a blinking unset VCR clock in Andy's living room, meticulous attention to detail creates the impression of a world with a sense of a past. Even though audiences have little time to register most of these grace notes, it was well worth it to the filmmakers to create the overall effect of a lived-in world.

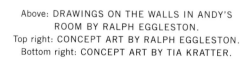

Above: DRAWINGS ON THE WALLS IN ANDY'S ROOM BY RALPH EGGLESTON.
Top right: CONCEPT ART BY RALPH EGGLESTON.
Bottom right: CONCEPT ART BY TIA KRATTER.

> "We wanted to do more dirt and dust bunnies—the stuff you really see in your house instead of some perfect place that exists inside a computer program."
>
> —RALPH EGGLESTON, Art Director

"Ralph Eggleston understands the life cycles of a vast
range of physical objects. He's good at imagining how
things age and how they wear. He's got a case history
in his head for every nail in the floor."

—TOM PORTER, Shader and Visual Effects Lead

A Great Story and Great Characters

"At the end of the day it's not the technique that the audience cares about; it's a great story, a visual feast, and great characters. They want to be taken on an emotional journey they've never been on before."

—PETER SCHNEIDER

The first step the *Toy Story* creators would take in making this film believable was to tell a strong, memorable story. Joe Ranft has compared the process of putting the story together for an animated feature film to peeling the layers of an onion. Each successive revision uncovers new issues to resolve as the story is gradually revealed. At the heart of *Toy Story* is the classic tale of two characters who cannot stand one another but who gradually come to form a lasting friendship.

STORYBOARD ART BY BUD LUCKEY.

Above and below right: TWO CONCEPTS OF ANDY BY STEVE JOHNSON.
Below left: STORYBOARD ART BY BUD LUCKEY.

"The bond Woody feels with Andy had to be the first thing we
got across in the movie. It had to be immediately tangible, or
you wouldn't care when something comes along and upsets it."

—ANDREW STANTON

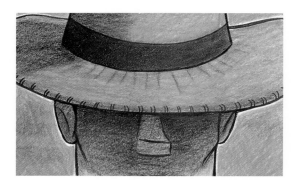

STORYBOARD ART BY JEFF PIDGEON
AND ROBERT LENCE.

Conjuring up a favorite toy who seemed worthy of Andy's love was no easy task. At first, Woody was not the lead character of *Toy Story* but instead was designated side-kick to Tinny, the star of Pixar's Academy Award®–winning short *Tin Toy*. As the story evolved from its original conception, it became clear that Tinny, a mute windup musician with a bright red marching cap, was too antiquated to serve as the main object of Andy's affections, and Woody became "Andy's favorite toy."

The filmmakers first envisioned the character as a wooden Charlie McCarthy–type ventriloquist's dummy that had once belonged to Andy's father. When Buzz the spaceman was introduced, the *Toy Story* creators changed their approach. "Since it was a buddy picture we wanted the dummy to be the complete opposite of a space toy, so we made him a cowboy," says Andrew Stanton. "Both genres complemented one another because each dealt with conquering some type of untamed frontier." Ultimately Woody underwent the

Left: CONCEPT ART BY JEFF PIDGEON.
Right: TINNY FROM *TIN TOY* (1988).

WOODY CONCEPT ART BY BUD LUCKEY.

final shift from ventriloquist's dummy to pull-string rag doll.

As Woody's look became more concrete, the *Toy Story* team sought Tom Hanks for the character's voice. Hanks's comic gifts brought an added dimension to the character, particularly when it came to expressing Woody's uniquely sarcastic personality. The casting also helped put across the concept of Andy's bedroom as a stable of wisecracking, decidedly unchildlike personalities, with Woody the governing emcee. Explains Joss Whedon, "Tom Hanks has a persona he brings with him—you know you're going to like him. You know that his values will end up being good, so even if he seems harsh, there's a point to it."

"On the surface Woody's very loose, very relaxed about everything. He sees himself as Mr. Nice Guy. But underneath he's thinking, who's my competition and what do I have to do to stay on top?"

—PETE DOCTER, Supervising Animator

Left: CONCEPT ART BY STEVE JOHNSON.
Above: CONCEPT ART BY BUD LUCKEY.

> "Buzz isn't like Andy's other toys. He believes he's the real Buzz Lightyear. He doesn't realize he's a mass-produced chunk of plastic standing on a kid's bedspread."
>
> —JASON KATZ, Story Artist

Above: BUZZ'S SPACESHIP PACKAGING BY BOB PAULEY.
Left: CONCEPT ART OF BUZZ GREETING THE INHABITANTS OF ANDY'S ROOM BY BUD LUCKEY.

> "John told us to think of Buzz as a cop who got a flat tire in Podunk on his way to save the galaxy."
>
> —ANDREW STANTON

Early in production, his name was Lunar Larry. But that somehow wasn't grand enough to suit the interstellar hotshot he became. Buzz Lightyear, as he was rechristened, fancies he's much more than a plastic replica of a TV network's idea of some moon-based patrolman: He believes he's here to save the universe.

Buzz was envisioned as the ultimate plaything you wished you could have as a kid. "We reached back to every favorite idea we could remember. And that of course had to involve outer space," says John Lasseter. The filmmakers reasoned first that Buzz's glow-in-the-dark frame would have to be strong enough to last through infinite vigorous missions. "We gave him all these great holes for screws and rivets, so there's no question in your mind exactly how he's put together," says Lasseter. From existing action figures, the designers appropriated arms with "karate-chop action." Since flying is high on every five-year-old boy's obsession list, Buzz sports pop-out wings with landing lights. On his wrist is a blinking laser (actually a little red lightbulb, as Woody likes to point out). Push the button on his chest, and out comes digitized, high-fidelity audio—"To infinity, and beyond!"—that puts Woody's scratchy pull-string voice box to shame.

Both Buzz's ultimate look and his vocal persona took time to nail down, but casting Tim Allen to voice Buzz helped the character to gel. "It took us a while to figure out that Buzz shouldn't come on like a superhero. He should be more like a cop," explains Andrew Stanton. The shift immediately helped to clarify how Buzz would be choreographed. As directing animator Rich Quade sees it, Buzz moves bluntly because that's the way he thinks: "He doesn't exactly have a keen sense of irony." Which makes him all the funnier, in story artist Jason Katz's view, since "the only universe Buzz patrols is in his head."

"The most fundamental story issue was figuring out the key to the relationship between Buzz and Woody."

—THOMAS SCHUMACHER

CONCEPT ART BY WILLIAM JOYCE.

WOODY CONCEPT ART BY BUD LUCKEY.

CONCEPT ART BY BUD LUCKEY.

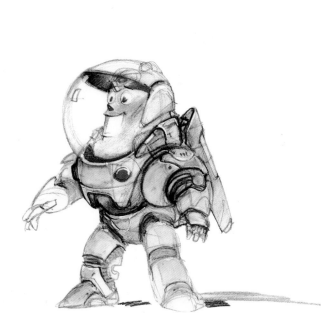

BY NILO RODIS.

BY WILLIAM JOYCE.

BY BUD LUCKEY.

BY BUD LUCKEY.

BY BUD LUCKEY.

BY BUD LUCKEY.

BY BUD LUCKEY.

BY JEFF PIDGEON.

"As in any great buddy movie, our two main characters are opposites and their dislike for each other grows out of that opposition."

—JOHN LASSETER

"Woody wanted to be a sarcastic guy, someone who hides his very real anxiety about being forgotten in a sort of malice and wisecracking. But for someone to write a pretty manipulative and self-serving character and make him attractive is a real tightrope walk."

—JOSS WHEDON, Screenwriter

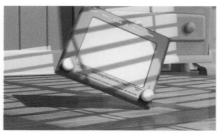

"Tom Hanks has the ability to make all kinds of emotions appealing. Even when he's yelling at somebody, he's likeable. That was crucial because Woody behaves pretty badly when he's not head toy anymore."

—JOHN LASSETER

"Buzz strides the shortest distance between two points. He's not one to waste energy."

—ASH BRANNON, Directing Animator

"Casting Tim Allen to voice Buzz gave us that quality we wanted of a macho guy with a soft underbelly. Tim's perfect at doing an everyday guy."

—JOHN LASSETER

Above: CONCEPT ART BY BOB PAULEY.

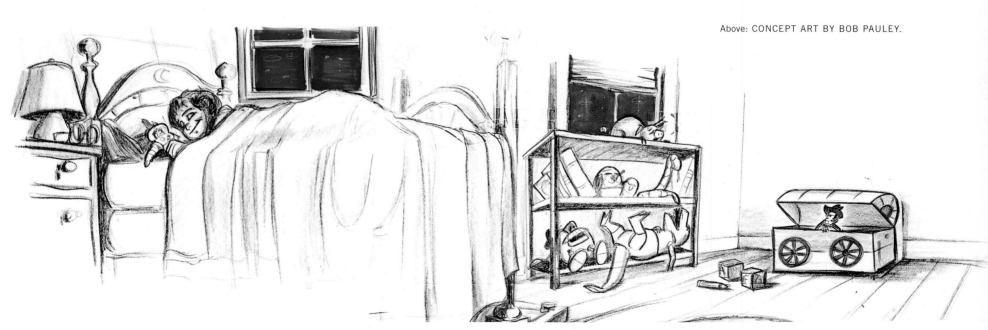

CONCEPT ART BY JILL CULTON.

CONCEPT ART BY BUD LUCKEY.

"Woody is the person who needs to learn the lesson of the movie. Buzz has something to learn in that he is really a toy and he's a little full of himself. But Woody is the one who needs to learn about friendship and trust and dealing with potential loss. He's the guy who needs to be redeemed."

—JOSS WHEDON

STORYBOARD ART BY BUD LUCKEY.

"Sid started out essentially as a surrogate for us to regress to being ten-year-olds. No big story arc for him, no agenda. We took what we knew about setting off cherry bombs and bugging our little sisters and all the stuff we did to our toys as kids, and rolled it into one character."

—JOHN LASSETER

Developing a villain, particularly when that villain is also a child, can be a tricky task. The question of just how evil to make Sid, the toys' nemesis, was one of the more difficult issues to be resolved in the making of *Toy Story*.

CONCEPT ART BY BOB McKNIGHT.

CONCEPT ART BY DAN HASKETT.

CONCEPT ART BY RALPH EGGLESTON.

CONCEPT ART BY BUD LUCKEY.

"When Sid hit his furthest-flung orbit of bad-boy extremity, some of the people at Disney said, 'This is a kid we don't recognize anymore. He needs to go back to being somebody people can look at and say, I knew a kid like this.'"

—JOHN LASSETER

CONCEPT ART BY RALPH EGGLESTON.

"Sid's personality was kind of hard to find, because nobody is out and out evil. In the end I think he's the character you identify with the most because he has a great imagination. And his imagination is the key to his voice. Because once you think of the games that he's playing, then he can be overtly malevolent and say evil things and rub his hands together and do his evil laugh because that's all part of the game."

—JOSS WHEDON

CONCEPT ART BY DAN HASKETT.

By toyland's moral compass, he's Victor Frankenstein and Dr. Moreau combined. But to his own way of thinking, Sid Philips (voiced by Erik Von Detten) is just your average preteen heavy-metal fan who likes to blow things up.

The filmmakers wrestled mightily with the issue of how movie audiences should view Sid. Combat Carl's death scene, in fact, is a nearly documentary reenactment of something Andrew Stanton once did to a toy in a field owned by his friend's family. "We made an M-80 into a little backpack for him," laughs Stanton. "I told John that story, and he said, okay, that's how we'll introduce Sid." Lasseter was equally inspired by Stanton's

account of "the time I tied an action figure to a rock at the beach and kept yelling, 'Talk! Tell us where the treasure is!' while the tide came in."

As the staff unleashed a flood of childhood exploits to pour into Sid, the struggle to make the character work with the overall story proved difficult. At one point the story team tried beefing up Sid into a full-tilt bullying nemesis for his neighbor Andy. They began generating scenarios of jealousy and rivalry between Sid and Andy, but that approach threw the plot line out of balance. Sid was taken "to just gruesome extremes," says Stanton. Various storyboards depicted him aiming staple guns, slingshots, and darts

at the hapless dolls. "He got so sadistic, it was as if he understood that these toys would feel the pain, or that they would suffer."

Ultimately it was felt that Sid should simply be someone who inadvertently causes huge obstacles for the story's real stars, Woody and Buzz. "It's their goal that matters most in the end," says Lasseter. "They're in peril and they want to get home. The drama was in seeing these typical things that kids do from a different perspective." In Lasseter's view, Sid is "just a typical aggressive boy who's playacting every time you hear him. He's not some stock nasty who wants to conquer the world. He's not Jafar. He's a child."

Modeling

Every animate creature in *Toy Story*, be it human, animal, or man-made plaything, had to be constructed in three dimensions in the computer as a "model" before it could be made to move, talk, blink, and come to life. Models were required, too, for every inanimate object that the characters pick up, touch, or ride in onscreen, as well as for nearly every structural and decorative feature of every environment the characters explore: lamps, tables, furniture, bed frames, hallways, staircases, whole buildings, even Sid's mom's clothesline.

In all, some 2,000 models were crafted for *Toy Story*. "Things that are rectilinear and geometric can be modeled easily and quickly using existing computer software," says animation scientist and modeler Eben Ostby. "But for models involving skin, or anything that looks like skin, we make an actual, real-world, clay reference sculpture before we build it in the computer." These sculptures help facilitate the complex custom modeling programming needed wherever there's fleshy physiology involved in a model. For that reason, busts were sculpted for the faces of Woody, Buzz, and almost all of *Toy Story*'s human characters, along with a complete head-to-toe casting for Sid's pit bull Scud.

Within the specialized subset of living

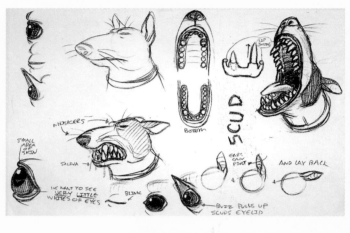
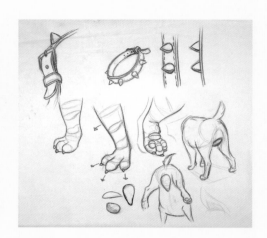

SCUD MODEL PACKET DRAWINGS, SHOWING DETAIL ABOUT HOW THE CHARACTER SHOULD LOOK AND MOVE, BY RALPH EGGLESTON.

characters, Scud was one of the most complex. "He's very compact, for one thing," says Ostby, "so his musculature had to be packed in tight. He has to do a lot of things, too. He has to appear to breathe hard, so his ribs expand and contract. He has to have working hip joints so his run is believable when he chases things. His body definitely has to appear very springy, very powerful. He doesn't have a subtle role. He's all teeth and snarls."

The myriad undulations that ripple through Scud's torso are called "deformations" (or "deforms" for short), and to get such flexibility into this "most deformative" of models, Ostby needed to "see the beast actually standing there" before he could capture him in programmer's language.

To accomplish this, the art department

began the task of making a Scud model with traditional tools. First they analyzed real-life canines and distilled the essence of live pit bulls into concept sketches. Then they shaped, in three ordinary dimensions, a full-blown, free-standing sculpture.

Scud leapt from the physical world into his first crude workstation-screen incarnation through the use of a pedestal-like contraption called the Polhemus Digitizer. Modelers can place a sculpture on this digitizing stand and point the end of a pencil-shaped wand at it, aiming briefly at each spot along a grid of intersecting lines penciled onto the sculpture's surface. A click of the keyboard translates that point in real space into a coordinate within a rectangular computer screen space, bound by axes for height, width, and depth.

Bill Reeves notes, "All the computer really does is record where the coordinate is that you have already established. You have to decide by eye how to lay in those lines on the sculpture in a pattern that's going to best suggest or describe the surface you want in mathematical terms." The grid points also have to fall in precisely those spots that the modeler will subsequently equip with "controls" called articulated variables, or "avars" for short, which the animators use to make model features like lips, cheeks, eyebrows, arms, legs,

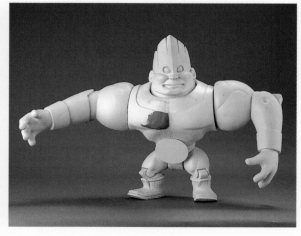

Left and right: SCULPTURES OF REX AND ROCKY GIBRALTAR BY NORM DeCARLO.

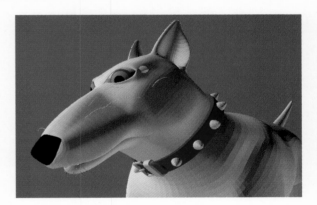

and ball-and-socket joints appear to pull, pucker, and otherwise function as if they had muscles inside and underneath them.

In effect, the modeler of a moving, living character is a digital-age marionette maker, attaching hundreds of interconnected "strings" that pull surfaces in concert to make them look alive. Scud, for instance, has a staggering 178 avars built into him. Ostby estimates that the animators used maybe three-quarters of these avars; the rest, including a battery of teeth avars to change shapes and positions, were needed for actually engineering Scud's contours in the first place. The animators did, however, make frequent use of Scud's "tummy" avars, tail-wag avars, leg

"rotators," and brow and cheek "puffers" (to make the skin scrunch in his jowls and forehead). Scud likes to scratch, too, which means "just about every part of his surface had to be equipped to deform," says Ostby.

Once the animators receive an approved model, they try to "break" it. "That means they'll push the avars to extremes to see if they can produce any unwanted cracks in the model's surface, or weird puckerings or buckles," says Ostby. "If so, it comes back to us for repairs." Because parts of the movie's story line were still in flux even as the modelers carried out their work, they had to guess their way through many design parameters. Says Reeves, "You always overmodel as a hedge against actions that haven't been thought up yet. But you've got to be careful because you could easily spend five years elaborating one model." Notes Ostby, "You're never really sure you're done until it's down the production line."

"Inevitably, these movies have to go through a death and a rebirth.
I don't know why, but I've never seen it where there's one pass
and everybody says, gee, that was easy."

—JOE RANFT, Story Co-creator

<hr />

Even the most creative storytellers in the world have to look at their story objectively and go through a process of revision. At Disney, in particular, stories undergo scrutiny and constant refining on the part of the creative team, often resulting in huge changes from early drafts. *Toy Story* would prove no exception.

"If the story isn't there, all the breakthrough computer graphics in the world piled onto it won't matter. You'll have made a piece of passing fashion."

—JOE RANFT

45

At the Burbank, California, studios of Walt Disney Feature Animation, they have nicknames for the moment of truth all good stories must face. "Black Monday," the *Aladdin* crew called it. *Lion King* staffers remember theirs as "the story meltdown."

What they're talking about is a day that seems to come partway through the creation of every contemporary animated Disney tale, a day that brings the realization that the narrative has critical weaknesses and that a good portion of it has to be changed.

For *Toy Story*'s creators, a "Black Monday" to call their own arrived on November 17,

1993. On that morning the key creative team working on the story sat down to view the first section of the movie in story reels, which are composed of story sketches that loosely approximate how the action will look in finished shots.

"The material doesn't really play as a movie until it's in reels," says Joe Ranft. "It's the first time you can assess the pacing and the story logic for its strengths and weaknesses."

Unfortunately, those gathered for the screening were hard-pressed to find any strengths at all. "It's almost embarrassing now to look at how far off we were in that original

take," says Andrew Stanton. Among the most glaring problems noted at the meeting:

—A take on Andy that wasn't very engaging. According to Stanton, "He was too deliberate in pushing Woody aside, instead of just overlooking his old favorite in his enthusiasm for Buzz."

—A confusing characterization for Buzz. "We made the mistake of not going 100 percent with his spaceman delusion," says Stanton. "He sort of knew he had an owner, and after he got lost, he wanted to get back to Andy just as much as Woody. That gave us two main characters with the same agenda."

But these missteps weren't nearly as serious

"We had 'sequence–itis.'
We'd been concentrating on one
scene at a time, polishing each one
out of order. They had a lot of
gags, but no flow. It was
depressing to all of us."

—ANDREW STANTON

or as offputting as one enormous, central mis-calculation. "We'd finally put Woody's scenes all together," says Ranft. "And he was a complete jerk." "He had to wind up being selfless by the story's end," says Stanton. "So our strategy had been, let's make him self*ish* in the beginning." As a result, Woody came off as a smug, sarcastic bully, lording his most-favored-plaything status over all the other toys.

"Then," says Stanton, "we made the ultimate character mistake." At what should have been a moment of maximum empathy for Woody, the audience instead got a display of utter venality: He deliberately pushes Buzz out

the window into Sid's yard, saying only, "Hey, it's a toy eat toy world."

This action rendered Woody's eventual repentance of absolutely no dramatic interest. "Wait, it gets worse!" Stanton laughs. "Then we had Woody be outright sadistic to Slinky on top of it all. He yells at him, 'Who said your job was to think, spring-weiner? If it wasn't for me, Andy wouldn't pay attention to you at all . . .' How could Sid's bedroom be any worse than Andy's at this point?"

It became clear to everyone present that the entire first half of the story would have to be reworked, and it was agreed that a new

A MEANER AND ROUGHER WOODY IN A
STORYBOARD BY BUD LUCKEY.

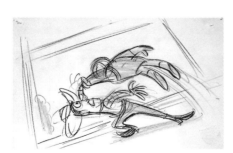

EARLY STORYBOARD SEQUENCE, IN WHICH WOODY DELIBERATELY THROWS BUZZ OUT THE WINDOW, BY ASH BRANNON AND MIKE CACHUELA.

"The Pixar team's willingness to go away and rethink ideas and throw things out is phenomenal. We would have a meeting where we'd say the relationship between these two characters is unsuccessful. Or we don't buy this moment of action. Or this isn't compelling enough. They are really fleet of foot like no one else and their ability to review things and turn them over is unlike anything we've seen."

—THOMAS SCHUMACHER

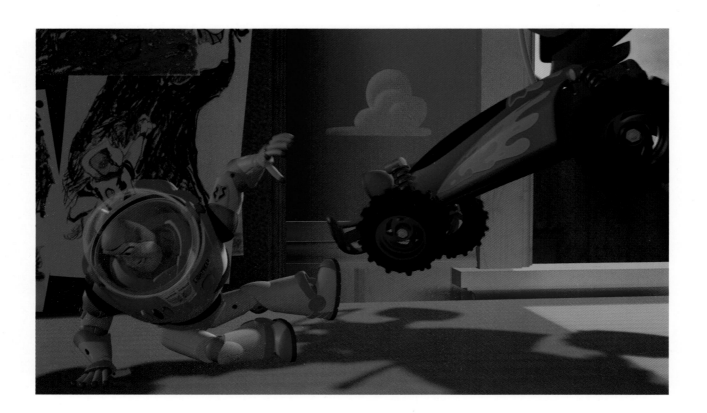

EARLY CONCEPT ART BY BUD LUCKEY.

version would be submitted by February 1994, a mere three months later. Faced with such fundamental problems, Ralph Guggenheim and Bonnie Arnold were forced to shut down animation—which had just begun in earnest—for several months. "If anybody helped us get back on the wagon most, it was the creative people at Disney," says Stanton. "Ron Clements and John Musker [co-directors of *Aladdin* and *The Little Mermaid*] were terrific. They immediately said, listen guys, you'll get through this. We went through it on *Aladdin*, and you'll turn it around."

In an astonishing burst of effort, that's exactly what the *Toy Story* team did. "We lived through Christmas that year working every weekend," Ranft recalls. "By February, it still wasn't all fixed, but everyone could see, okay, this is now on track."

Woody and Andy got a new scene together at the start of the movie to better establish the bond between them. And a montage keyed to a new Randy Newman tune, "Strange Things," made Woody's situation much more poignant and empathetic. "That's the sequence where you now totally understand Woody's jealousy," says Ranft. And that's why, at the moment Buzz sails out the window *by accident* in the revised story line, you in fact feel sorriest for Woody, whose shame and anger have pushed him into making a mistake. "It's a moment like a lot of people have in childhood, where you took a whack at your sister or you wanted to get back at some kid and they actually got hurt," Ranft speculates. "Instead of turning the audience off, it brings them right in on Woody's side."

Looking back on all the challenges, the story staffers seem resigned to the fact that when it comes to crafting animation plotlines, endurance and persistence count more than anything else. "The one luxury with animation is that you can board it again and again and again," says Stanton. "We just found out the hard way that the one thing we did right was we were willing to cut stuff no matter how funny and just keep going and try it again."

"The main thing is, you can't fall in love with your ideas. It takes stamina to keep that in mind when you're reboarding something for the fiftieth time. You get to feel like a boxer rising up off the canvas."

—ROBERT LENCE, Story Supervisor

STORYBOARD ART BY KELLY ASBURY.

50

A Visual Feast

"We're the first step in taking the movie from a two-dimensional plan to a three-dimensional world."

—EWAN JOHNSON, Layout Lead

When you're making a computer animated film, mapping out the action in words and in rough drawings raises as many questions as it settles about how the sequence will actually look shot by shot. Before animators can begin working on bringing the characters to life, the layout artists work to bring the film one step closer to the screen. It is the members of the layout department, working closely with the director and editorial team, who determine where exactly characters will stand and from what angle we will view them; what objects will be beside, in front of, and behind the figures; and how many close-ups, medium shots, and long shots are needed to keep the action clear, while packing maximum dramatic punch.

Ralph Guggenheim calls layout "ground zero in the manufacturing process" of creating each finished shot. For most of *Toy Story*'s production schedule, the work of translating story sketches to specific shots fell to supervising lead artist Craig Good, lead layout artists Ewan Johnson and Kevin Bjorke and later to layout artists Desiree Mourad and Roman Figun.

As Good describes it, "If you took a live-action director of photography and sawed him in half, we'd be the part that worries about the camera." Good talks about using cameras

quite literally, but of course there is no actual camera in computer animation. The "viewfinder" is a computer workstation viewscreen, and what it "looks" out at is controlled by menu commands that position and steer a simulated camera "lens" through a "set" modeled entirely in a computer environment.

Good and Johnson conferred constantly with director Lasseter and with editors Bob Gordon and Lee Unkrich to ensure that all the individual snippets they blocked out would play together smoothly. As the layout team blocked simplified versions of the characters

into initial poses that would later be brought to life by the animators, they weren't moving them across flat backgrounds. They had to place the character models in space, in performance areas where the apparent depth and width could change radically depending on where and how they used their "camera."

The layout department's first pass was a nerve-wracking moment in the making of each sequence, because there were often rude surprises in store. The actual scale of the sets and characters didn't always match up with what the story artists had sketched because

"Once we started lining up a scene's shot list with editorial, the storyboards would pretty much get tossed. The storyboards were designed for one purpose: to communicate the plot and the gags quickly and simply. They aren't designed to be blueprints. They're more like advice."

—CRAIG GOOD, Supervising Layout Lead

"they can cheat things," says Good. The layout team also had to find artful ways to "cheat" the apparent scale of the environment—and no scene tested that skill more than Woody's attempt to get rid of Buzz atop Andy's desk. "Buzz had to break into a full run along that desktop," says Johnson. "But the desk wasn't very large." Artful editing helped, but the main solution was to model a second, larger desktop "just for the shots where you're up on top of it, so it's two different sizes depending on where you see it from."

Because computer animation creates fully dimensional settings, the layout team's "camera" could go above, below, in and around the action as well as simply stand still. "Our camera could do anything a real one could and then some," says Good. That enabled layout to program in a tilt up or down, a pan, a track alongside something, or a dolly forward or back, as well as to pivot the base of the camera body itself on any number of axes as it made one of those major moves.

Keeping the camera moves as simple as

possible was part of a conscious effort to make the audience feel like they're watching a typical live-action movie, not a piece of technical wizardry. That conservative approach, in Good's view, is essential for drawing audiences into the story's emotional core. "You don't want gimmicks," he says. "There's already gimmickry enough in the fact that this is the first film of its kind. You don't want the way you treat the camera to be so strange that it reminds people of that novelty when they should be getting into the story."

"It's not like drawn animation, where you have to paint a new background every time you want a different angle. Our sets get built once, to fixed dimensions. As you position and move your camera, you see the changing view you'd have walking through an actual physical space."

—BILL REEVES, Supervising Technical Director

Above: STORYBOARD ART BY JOE RANFT.
Top: STORYBOARD ART BY BUD LUCKEY.

"It's easy to draw a perfectly convincing pose of Woody putting his arm around Slinky's shoulder and talking in his ear. But try setting that up with your final character models where Woody is three times taller than Slinky, and there goes your gag. We have to come up with solutions for those kinds of problems all the time."

—CRAIG GOOD

Rex

"It's gonna be me, I know it. I'm the logical choice; I'm already extinct."

"It's my unmanly forearms. They say 'Hello! Forgot to evolve!' I can't even touch my nose."

REX CONCEPT ART BY BUD LUCKEY.
EARLY SCRIPT LINES BY JOSS WHEDON.

His body is molded in the image of the most fearsome carnivore the earth has ever known. But nervous, garrulous Rex, says John Lasseter, doesn't fit that skin at all: The guy's a "cream puff" trapped in a monster's body.

The director felt he wanted to include a dinosaur "because every kid has one," yet he also wanted to play the character against type. During the production's development stages, Joe Ranft kept pondering those weak little arms T. Rexes have. One day, he caricatured the animal arching his eyebrows and anxiously wringing his two feeble hands—and Rex was born.

Rex's physical persona met its match when Lasseter cast Wallace Shawn as his voice. The diminutive actor, best known for sputtering "Inconceivable!" in *The Princess Bride*, instantly made Rex one neurotic reptile. "Wally couldn't play Rex fearsome if he wanted to," says Lasseter. "That was ideal. Because 'poor Rex,' as we call him, is completely insecure. He's not comfortable with his calling. He's always trying to be the tyrannosaurus he thinks everybody expects, but he can't quite do it."

Lasseter insisted that Rex always be made to move and act like the cheaply constructed plaything he is. Says the director, "We certainly had the ability to animate him with all the articulation a real beast would have, but he's a rigid plastic toy. So when his legs move, they only move around the given rotation points that are manufactured into him. When he turns his head, the whole head top rotates, because there's a seam around his neck. And as soon as he does that, the spray-paint markings don't line up anymore, so he's as unconvincing to see as he is to hear."

Guionne LeRoy, who animated the bulk of Rex's shots along with Jeff Pidgeon and Karen Kiser, delighted in giving Rex crude mouth movements to match his simple hinged jaw, and relied on Rex's "pathetic" arms for comic effects. "He can't really shrug, but you can get around that with the way he holds those bony fingers," Kiser says.

The story staff didn't always take the character's stunted appendages into account: They sent the animators many Rex gags that proved anatomically impossible in three dimensions. Rex couldn't scurry up a table and knock over a walkie-talkie during Andy's birthday party; he had to shake the table off-camera instead. He couldn't easily hug anybody either, or hold a flashlight, or hand a chain of plastic monkeys out the window. No matter, says Andrew Stanton, "we just kept giving him less action and more punch lines."

Left: CONCEPT ART BY WILLIAM JOYCE.
Center: CONCEPT ART BY BUD LUCKEY.

"For the audience to believe in them, Woody and Buzz have to look like they're thinking. Only animators who are great actors can give you that."

—JOHN LASSETER

With story ideas in place, dialogue recorded, layouts determined, and models ready, it was next the task of the animators to bring the characters to life. Animators from all fields of animation—two-dimensional drawn animation, puppet, clay animation, model and a select few from computer graphics—were brought to work on *Toy Story*. Some of the film's youthful team of animators had never so much as clicked on a mouse; many received training in the tools of computer animation as they were brought to the production.

CONCEPT ART OF THE DINOCO GAS STATION BY RALPH EGGLESTON.

"So many of the animators were working in the computer medium for the first time.
It doesn't matter if they use a pencil or a machine or a puppet, a good animator is a good animator."

—KATHLEEN GAVIN, Vice President of Production for Special Projects, Walt Disney Feature Animation

Ask the *Toy Story* animation staff about which scene in the movie best showcases their art and an almost unanimous verdict emerges: It's when Woody and Buzz fight amid the towering gas pumps of a "Dinoco" gas station.

"It really gets across their relationship," says Mark Oftedal, who animated many of Woody's manic outbursts in the showdown. "You've been seeing the tension between them build and build, and once they're alone together, it explodes.

"When we planned it, John was clear that he wanted Woody still sort of dumbfounded that Buzz still thinks he's a spaceman, until the instant he screams at him, 'YOU . . . ARE . . . A . . .TOOOOOY!' The idea was to pop Woody right into the screaming. You don't see

WOODY EXPLODES AT BUZZ, SCREAMING "YOU ARE A TOY!!!"

it coming. It's funnier and punchier that way."

Indeed, the moment is so punchy it knocked the film's story staff for a loop the first time they watched it in rough animation. "We weren't prepared for how much stronger it played than what we'd imagined," says Andrew Stanton. "We'd gotten used to thinking, after a lot of boards, that these were

cartoon characters. But they're not; they look like they're made of plastic and fabric and they actually exist."

Part of what makes the gas station scene such a tour de force of character animation is that even as Woody and Buzz harangue each other verbally, they're speaking two contrapuntal body languages. Woody moves like the

STORYBOARD ART BY JEFF PIDGEON.

AND WHEN WE GET THERE...   BE ABLE TO FIND...   TRANSPORT YOU...   HOME!   PAUSE (F 121 D 140)

THUMBNAIL SKETCHES WERE USED BY SOME ANIMATORS AS A VISUAL REFERENCE,
WHILE OTHERS RELIED ON ACTING OUT THE SCENES. SKETCHES BY GLEN McQUEEN.

flimsiest conceivable rag doll—he's boneless. When his temper flares, his legs buckle and his arms thrash like out-of-control fire hoses. The more he loses command of the situation, the floppier he gets. The animation also makes it comically clear that Woody is literally a lightweight: One right hook from Buzz and he flies across the asphalt.

"Structurally, Buzz is the total opposite," says directing animator Ash Brannon, who handled the punching shots. "Except for his squeaky-soft face, he's made of hard plastic." That rigidity suits Buzz's persona perfectly: Stiff, methodical and unironic, he's a by-the-

book type of guy. The basic visual shorthand the animators kept in mind all through the production was, think klutzy curves for Woody poses; think athletic angles for Buzz.

To find the right look for Woody's movements, the animators studied footage of loose-limbed actor Ray Bolger (the scarecrow in *The Wizard of Oz*) as well as reference videotapes of Tom Hanks reading his *Toy Story* lines. The exploits of movie and TV superheroes served as useful inspirations for Buzz. More often than not, however, the *Toy Story* animators wound up caricaturing their own physical tics and idiosyncracies. When it

came time to execute a shot alone at a computer workstation with perhaps only a mirror for physical reference, the animator's own head turn or leg kick or karate chop became the final guide.

In a departure from traditional Disney practice, the *Toy Story* animators shared duties on all of the characters rather than each focusing on just one. Nevertheless, specialties developed as Lasseter cast the animators for specific scenes that reflected their individual personality quirks. Lanky Doug Sweetland was assigned to animate what his colleagues call the "spastic flailer" shots because he's a bit hyperactive himself. Rich Quade, who's known around the studio as a thoughtful and laid-back figure, was assigned many of Woody's quieter emotional scenes. And cutup Glen McQueen, who can reduce spectators to helpless laughter with a deadpan expression, was the undisputed champ at bringing out Woody's insincere side.

58

"We never thought Woody and Buzz's repartee would hold the spotlight in and of itself. But once they were animated, suddenly the chemistry between them was the highlight of the movie."

—ANDREW STANTON

STORYBOARD ART BY BUD LUCKEY.

"The animator knows the art of making something come alive. But there's an art to building the models themselves. There's artistry in getting the lighting and the surfaces right, and getting the hair and the texture right, and having that bed quilt bounce up and down exactly as you'd expect it to."

—EDWIN CATMULL, President, Pixar

To create truly artful computer-produced graphics it's essential to assign top-flight technicians and programmers—people like Pixar's Bill Reeves, Eben Ostby, Darwyn Peachey, and Tom Hahn—to the task of creating the best, simplest computer animation tools, not choreographing the final action. Then those tools are given to people whose keenest interest lies in figuring out how a dog trots or how a doll face takes a punch, rather than in devising lines of code.

"The models for the characters are created by somebody else. They're there. I never have to worry that Woody's head is suddenly looking a little too big, or that I didn't draw it square enough from this angle. That's a given. All I have to do is make it move."

—RICH QUADE, Directing Animator

"In computer animation, you've got a built-in level of reality that is not there in a graphic medium," Pete Docter says. "There's a lot of visual shorthand you can use when you depict a figure with a pencil and paper. In computer animation, your character has highly realistic shading and lighting and shadows and high-

lights and a sense of solidity. It's a 3-D object, not a cartoon."

Ironically, the animators take their first step toward building a mood of realism by plunging into complete abstraction. When they begin their work, the figures they manipulate are no more than skinned, stripped-down

versions of the highly realistic computer "models" built by the technical staff for each character. "When we animate Woody, he's made up of cylinders and he has no real face," says Docter. "He's just a sphere head."

Using these crude analogues, the computer can redraw each frame fast enough to let the

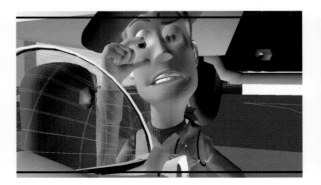
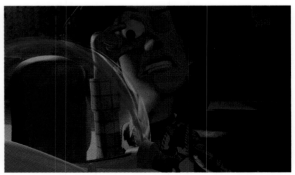

Left to right: WOODY AND BUZZ AS STAND-IN MODELS, FULL MODELS WITH AMBIENT LIGHTING, AND FULLY RENDERED.

ANIMATOR'S WORKSTATION DISPLAY.

artists make comparisons between frames. As animators compose shots of Woody running, for example, they key the appropriate numbers into columns of avars, which operate the simulated "muscles" that control a particular motion. If the computer were to render each position in full detail, the process would bog down so much that before long, the animator would lose the feel of the overall movement. With the simplified shapes, though, the computer zips along. Within seconds, it stores the individual frames and plays them back as normal, fluid motion; the artists can see almost instantly the moves they've created.

Once they've finished prodding and refining all the positions for every limb in each frame of a shot, the animators command their terminals to turn back on the "pats," or complete surface data, for such elements as Woody's eyelids, facial features, neckerchief, and so forth. The frames are then downloaded to another machine, where they can be played back at standard speed.

The go-ahead to execute a "pats-on" version, however, comes only after the animators sit down with Lasseter and view the initial "polygons" and motion test "blocking" in daily screening sessions. Critiques and comments of the director and fellow animators gathered during these screenings prompt meticulous reworking and improvement of each shot.

Because all of the staff's decisions about how well a performance works have to be made while staring at highly abstracted versions of the characters, *Toy Story* boasts a certain purity of choreographic style. "It actually helps a lot to have to make your acting work without a face," says Pete Docter. "You wind up doing much more full-bodied pantomime."

"If a character doesn't move across the room much the way you're used to seeing people move in a million real-life situations, suddenly it breaks down. You're constantly meeting a much higher level of disbelief in the audience."

—PETE DOCTER

Top right and bottom left: STORYBOARD ART BY BUD LUCKEY.

Above: CONCEPT ART OF THE INTERIOR OF THE PIZZA PLANET DELIVERY SHUTTLE BY TIA KRATTER.
Overleaf: CONCEPT ART BY RALPH EGGLESTON.

"If you take away the characters' surfaces, all you're left with to get across your meaning is movement and timing. There aren't any of the concerns that a graphic animator has, of how to caricature a three-dimensional object in two dimensions. We're building shots purely out of actions, and that's fine because that's the essence of animation."

—RICH QUADE

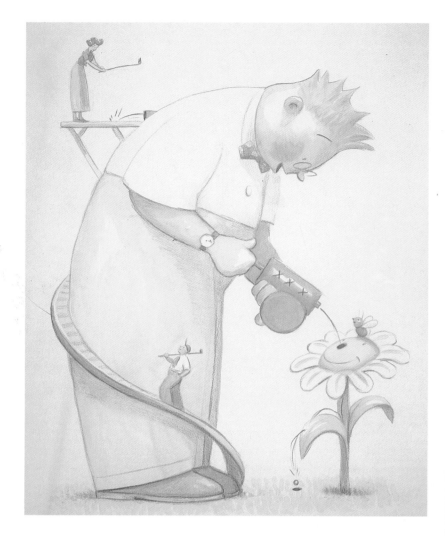

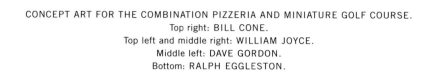

CONCEPT ART FOR THE COMBINATION PIZZERIA AND MINIATURE GOLF COURSE.
Top right: BILL CONE.
Top left and middle right: WILLIAM JOYCE.
Middle left: DAVE GORDON.
Bottom: RALPH EGGLESTON.

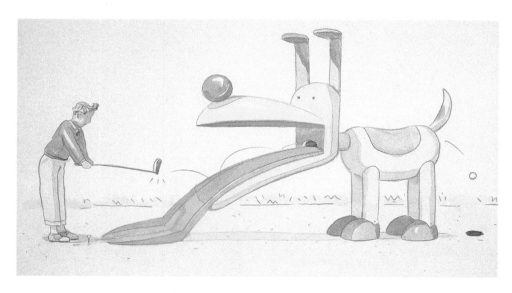

"To our way of thinking, we build real sets. They just happen to exist in virtual space instead of physical space. You've got to keep that live-action outlook in your head if you want this to look like an actual working place, and not some perfect hermetically sealed illustration."

—DAMIR FRKOVIC, Modeler

The creation of sets in computer animation starts in the art department where concepts and ideas are developed through two-dimensional conceptual drawings, paintings, and sketches. Each set design, like every created object in *Toy Story*, is then made into a model packet—a set of more or less refined blueprints that guide the modeler in the construction of the virtual set. Careful attention is paid, not only to how the characters will move and interact with their environment, but to the overall impact that environment will have on the mood of the scene.

STORYBOARD ART BY KELLY ASBURY.

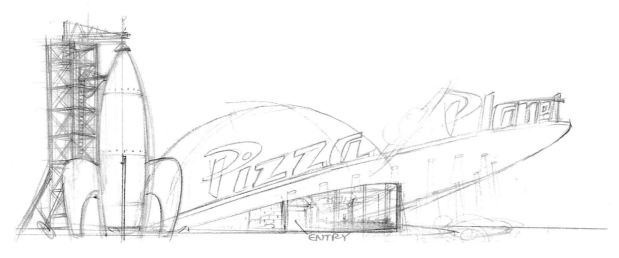

MODEL PACKET DRAWING OF THE PIZZA PLANET EXTERIOR BY BILL CONE.

The design, everyone agreed, was spectacular on paper: a wild pastiche of '50s drive-in diners, '90s video arcades, and futuristic science fiction movie motifs. The story department had only come up with the space-age diner idea after devoting months to a different concept: a combination pizzeria and miniature golf course. But the golf gag scenes built around that location were not working well with the development of the Buzz Lightyear character. A decision was made to scrap the whole putt-putt scenario in favor of a fast-food environment that Buzz could perceive as a space port.

The idea of an interstellar fast-food fueling station so fired up the art department that the old settings were reworked at near light speed. A concept art team led by Ralph Eggleston, Bob Pauley, and Bill Cone incorporated themed details into plans for the new site, filling a game arcade with inspired made-up machinery, and turning the restaurant's interior dome into a starry planetarium ceiling.

Modeler Damir Frkovic's task was to

Above: STORYBOARD ART OF VARIOUS ARCADE
GAME CONCEPTS BY JASON KATZ.
Right: MODEL PACKET DRAWING OF PIZZA
PLANET EXTERIOR BY BILL CONE.

"We suddenly realized, we've got a delusional
astronaut, so why not make the restaurant a place he
mistakes for a space port? It seems so obvious now,
such a natural link with the rest of the story, it's hard
to believe Pizza Planet was an eleventh-hour change."

—ANDREW STANTON

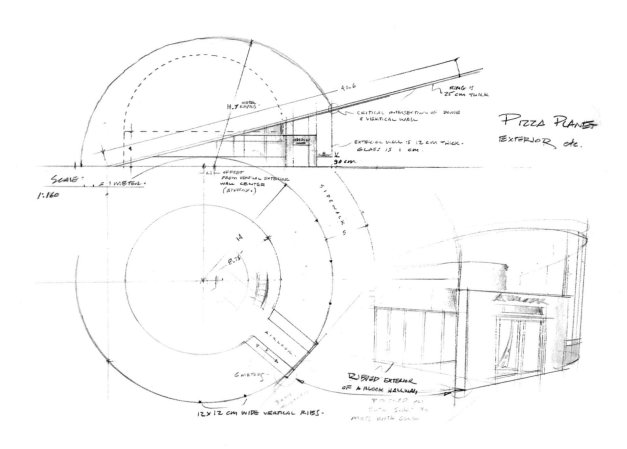

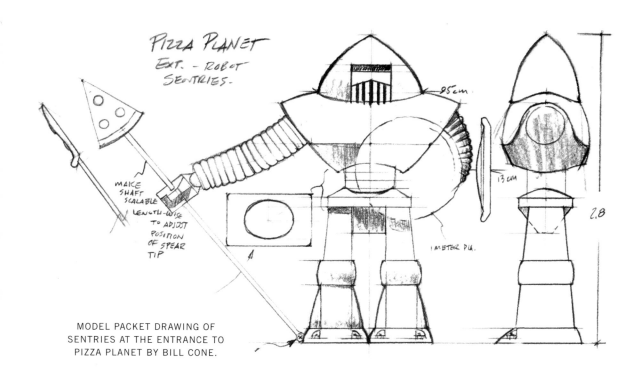

MODEL PACKET DRAWING OF
SENTRIES AT THE ENTRANCE TO
PIZZA PLANET BY BILL CONE.

translate Cone's detailed hand-drawn room
schematics of each beam, floor tile, and wall
panel into an elaborate computer realm construction job. As with any construction project, the Pizza Planet specs envisioned in two
dimensions didn't always work so well in
three. Frkovic had to do some fiddling with
the restaurant's proportions to keep them
pleasingly spherical, yet he also pushed its
shape in ways impossible with an actual set.
Says Frkovic, "In terms of structural integrity,
we cheat a lot. That big enormous neon 'Pizza
Planet' sign on top of the rings would break
right through the roof if you built it the way
we show it."

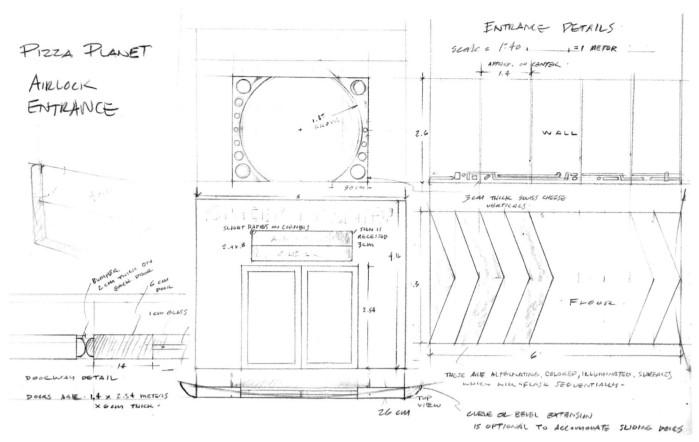

PIZZA PLANET
AIRLOCK
ENTRANCE

Above and right: MODEL PACKET DRAWINGS OF THE PIZZA
PLANET ENTRANCE AND AIRLOCK BY BILL CONE.

"When we build an elaborate environment like Pizza Planet the art department acts as the architectural firm. Whoever takes their plans and turns them into a working set acts as the one-man construction crew."

—DAMIR FRKOVIC

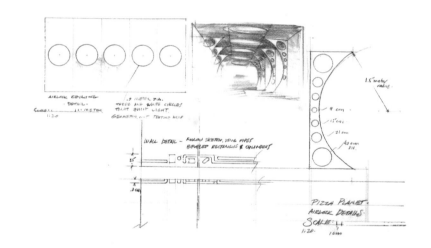

Frkovic's sense of craft, too, helped provide a convincing filigree in details the art department might not have had time or inspiration to specify in their "model packet" instructions. In Frkovic's mind, whether he wields a blade or a keypad, the task remains the same. "I add lots of little detailing that nobody tells me to do," he explains. "It's always the goal to add that little layer to make the set look less perfect, less of the computer world and more like a messy, believable place."

MODEL PACKET DRAWING OF THE PLANET KILLER
ARCADE GAME BY BOB PAULEY.

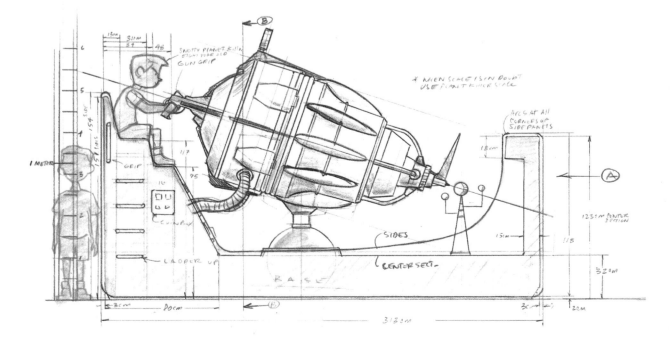

Above and top: STORYBOARD ART BY JASON KATZ.

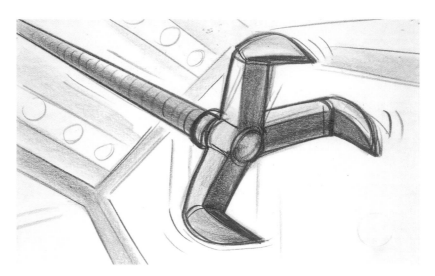

THE "CLAW." STORYBOARD ART BY JOE RANFT.

Above, from top: STORYBOARD ART BY
JASON KATZ (top and bottom), BUD LUCKEY,
ANDREW STANTON, AND JILL CULTON.
Opposite: STORYBOARD ART BY KELLY ASBURY.

Story Session

"Somebody said 'the claw' and the room just exploded with people all jabbering ideas at once. We had our scene in that instant."
—ANDREW STANTON

GAG SESSION BOARDS BY CHRIS SANDERS.

While the art department and the technicians designed models and sets, and the animators set to work on scenes already locked down and laid out, there were still story ideas in development. Some of the most memorable moments in the film would result from a meeting in Burbank with Pixar's story team and a group of the most creative Disney artists in attendance. Gathered at Walt Disney Studios on October 10, 1994, were John Lasseter, Andrew Stanton, story supervisior Robert Lence, Pete Docter, Joe Ranft, and story artists Jason Katz and Jill Culton along with a dozen seasoned Disney animators, directors, and story artists. Together they hoped they could shore up certain weak narrative spots. Time was growing short in the production schedule, and remaining story issues had to be settled quickly. Total time allotted to generate definitive progress: one hour.

Disney Feature Animation had convened many such brain-trust sessions before, but never with an outside collaborator. Among the dozen top creative artists present from Disney were animators Will Finn (who supervised work on *Aladdin*'s Iago) and Randy Cartwright (*Aladdin*'s Magic Carpet); top story and conceptual artists Joe Grant (*Snow White* and *Dumbo*), Barry Johnson (*The Lion King*), and Chris Sanders (*The Lion King*); directors Rob Minkoff and Roger Allers (*The Lion King*), and

Kirk Wise and Gary Trousdale (*Beauty and the Beast* and *The Hunchback of Notre Dame*).

The *Toy Story* team's biggest worry that day was what to do about the scene in which Buzz tumbles into a coin-operated game filled with little Pizza Planet mascots. "We'd already tried having them be little bears and little slices of pizza with sunglasses," says Jason Katz. "But we'd finally settled on the game being a big rocket ship with spacemen inside, to give Buzz a reason to be drawn to it." What to do, though, with those aliens? Session after session back at Pixar had

"With the people in that room that day, you could have been talking about drywall and you would have gotten the best drywall gags in the world."
—ROBERT LENCE

yielded no usable gags or character design.

At first, no promising solutions emerged. Then somebody—it might have been Trousdale, but no one seems to remember for sure—said the words "the claw." Suddenly pencils flew over sketchpads. Ideas tumbled out in a rush. Why not make the game's mechanical pick-up mechanism the center of the little alien toys' world? "We began batting back and forth every mindless sect out of every movie we could think of," says Stanton. "Don't fight the claw, do the will of the claw, and on and on." "We started talking about South American cargo cults," adds John Lasseter. "These aliens had never been in the outside world, so they might be like those rain forest tribes who see a plane and wind up worshipping it as a deity."

Chris Sanders was the first to whip out a drawn design for the squeeze toys—three eyes, one antenna—and it survives more or less intact in the finished scene. "I think the idea that they should be really squeaky toys came up right then, too," says Lasseter. "It was just one great touch after another." In only a few minutes, a story logjam that hadn't been broken in months of effort suddenly yielded. "The amazing thing is," says Katz, "the Pizza Planet scenes feel just as strong and as integral as other sequences we took great pains to develop over many, many weeks."

STORYBOARD ART.
First row; second row, right; and fourth row: JILL CULTON.
Second row, left: BUD LUCKEY. Third row, left: JASON KATZ. Third row, right: JEFF PIDGEON.

To set foot in Sid Philips's lair is to enter a computer-rendered room knee-deep in life-like dirt, dust, and clutter. A veritable indoor landfill, the place is layered with soda cans, discarded food, magazines, and probably heaps of dirty clothes—if you could find them under the debris. Part of the unkempt ambience stems from the tortured shape of the room itself. "It's got a jumble of oddly intersecting roof planes," says Bill Cone, who based his design for the space on a misbegotten attic that Pete Docter had been renovating. "I never would have thought of cutting up a roofline that way. It gives an off-kilter feeling, like you can't orient yourself." Eben Ostby, who translated Cone's schematic drawings into a computer-rendered space, agrees that "it's the most bizarre

configuration I built in the whole movie."

Yet the most atmospheric elements in Sid's sanctum sanctorum are the implements of destruction and mischief strewn around the room, and for these, Ostby claims no credit. "I'm not the decorator for the house," he says. "I'm just the contractor. I lay the floors, put up the walls and the ceilings, and that's it."

The task of filling in those bare spaces with disarray fell to animation scientist Kelly O'Connell. Like everyone involved in *Toy Story*, O'Connell talks about her computer realm props exactly as if she'd been working on a live-action movie—but there are differences. In real-world moviemaking, set dressers buy or fabricate suitable items and simply put them in place with their own hands. When you're

appointing a virtual homestead, the process isn't so straightforward.

Guided by lists from the art department, the modeling staff first created an inventory of objects. Sid's room contains coils of barbed wire, "crushed and uncrushed" cans and cups, cassette tapes, spring-loaded mousetraps, assorted knives, matches "regular and burnt," darts, pencils (mostly stuck in the ceiling), bumper stickers, and over a hundred pieces of crumpled paper. Along the shelves stand rows of jars with icky substances in them. "I don't even know what some of them are," O'Connell confesses. O'Connell took special care to find spots for a few crowning pieces: a lava lamp with doll heads floating inside, assorted Day-Glo posters, and two "torture devices" on Sid's

The environment designed for Sid had to reflect his distinctively imaginative personality. Littered as it was by every conceivable kind of clutter, Sid's room provided an opportunity for the craft of *Toy Story* animation scientist Kelly O'Connell to shine as she strove to make the environment reflect the inner workings of Sid's mind.

Above: STORYBOARD ART BY ANDREW STANTON.
Opposite: CONCEPT OF SID'S HOUSE BY BILL CONE.

Above and right: THE WALLS OF SID'S ROOM ARE ADORNED WITH DAY-GLO POSTERS LIT BY A LAVA LAMP AND BLACK LIGHT.

desk—a waffle iron and a board with nails sticking out of it.

Taking her cues from sketches by Ralph Eggleston, O'Connell positioned each bit of bric-a-brac using a menu-driven system that required specifying three numerical coordinates for each placement. "The hardest thing in the world to do with the computer is make things look like they fell at random," says O'Connell.

The chief problem in crafting sloppy piles is "intersection," where one object appears to cut right through the surface of another. "Modeled objects aren't solid, they're just information in the computer," says O'Connell. "There's nothing to tell the edges to bounce off each other. As soon as you start piling things at odd angles, it gets hard to keep them distinct." Part of O'Connell's job lies in artfully hiding spots where two or more objects occupy the same virtual space. "There are thousands of intersections in this room," she admits. "Hopefully you won't see them, because they're all hidden under the objects at the tops of the piles."

Every texture and surface pattern in the room—the simulated grain of the fake wood paneling, the relief in the velveteen wallpaper, the weave of the sculptured avocado carpeting, the knife marks in the windowsills—was applied by shader and visual effects lead Tom Porter.

75

CONCEPT ART OF SID'S ROOM BY STEVE JOHNSON.

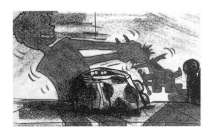

"You can bet the carpet hasn't
been vacuumed in years."

—RALPH EGGLESTON

DOLL'S HEAD IN A MAYONNAISE JAR.
ART BY TIA KRATTER.

Like some ultimate contact paper manufacturer, he takes flat, surface-pattern visual information, then writes a customized mathematical "shader" program to "wrap" it around the three-dimensional geometry of a modeled object. Before Porter worked on it, Sid's room looked like a collection of smooth, abstracted shapes; when he was done, the place overwhelmingly conjured the wretched, stuck-in-the-'70s mood that

Eggleston was looking for—right down to the bits of glitter in the stucco ceiling.

Many surfaces in the movie had to be created by hand by the art department. "They don't usually paint realistic copies of marble patterns, or wood, or plasterboard because we have that information available to us," says Porter. "They much more often add scruffy touches like spills and scratches, because I can't easily program in a drip or a soda stain." Sid's desk, for instance, boasts four separate layers of hand-depicted detail: a "splatter" layer of paint marks, a "bump map" where the artists imagine Sid hit it with hammers or scraped it with blades, a "specularity" layer to specify where light is more or less reflective around those pocks and irregularities, and a "dirt" layer for general grunge.

The shader program then instructs these

layers to "talk" to each other in ways that mimic the play of light over real objects. Because this information exists as component layers, says Bob Pauley, "There's tremendous control. You can improve on just one element in isolation from any of the others to achieve what you want."

The catch for the background artists, says Tia Kratter, is that only in the final composite computer images do these layers look like recognizable things. "You're painting sculpturally," she explains. "You're painting for information more than appearance so a lot of what you do doesn't look like anything but total abstraction." Kratter also points out, "You have no portfolio of finished backgrounds when you're done. Painters are going to leave this film saying, 'Well, here's this dirt layer I painted for the dents in Sid's mailbox.'"

CONCEPT ART BY BILL CONE.

SOME OF THE POSTERS CREATED FOR THE WALLS OF SID'S ROOM.
ART BY BOB PAULEY, BILL CONE, AND TIA KRATTER.

"My job was to arrange stuff you knew a kid like Sid would like. Dirty, messy, dangerous—anything disgusting and awful would be perfect for Sid's room."

—KELLY O'CONNELL, Animation Scientist

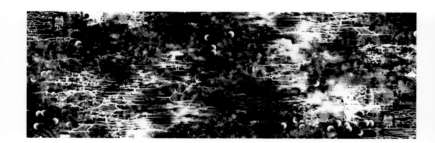

Above: SID'S DESK FULLY RENDERED.
Left, top to bottom: BUMP MAP, SPECULARITY LAYER, AND COLOR LAYER.
CONCEPT ART FOR SHADER PROGRAM FOR SID'S DESK
BY TIA KRATTER AND TOM PORTER.

Last to be developed, but hardly of least importance in the *Toy Story* pantheon, are the natives of Sid's lair. Collectively known to the creative team as the "mutant toys," these pieced-together characters are as much the twisted creations of the filmmakers' minds as they are the fictional products of Sid's imagination.

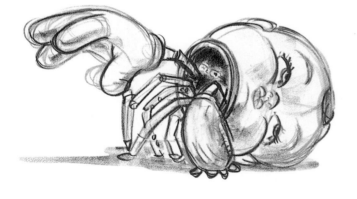

"The mutants are never inherently scary just to look at; after all, they're supposed to turn out to be helpful. They're simply supposed to look like toys ripped apart by a bratty, bullying kid."

—RALPH EGGLESTON

Above: CONCEPT ART BY BOB PAULEY.
Opposite: CONCEPT ART BY KEVIN HAWKES.

Creepy is the word for the audience's first glimpse of "Babyhead," crawling from under Sid's mattress on arachnoid, erector-set legs. He's a walking witness to Sid's contempt for toys. "I want people to think when they first see them that these guys are scarier than hell," says Lasseter.

Through pages upon pages of early concept designs by artists Bud Luckey and Bob Pauley, as well as by Joe Ranft and Jeff Pidgeon, the "Frankenstein feeling" Lasseter was seeking eluded him. "They were so darn cute," laughs the director. "They were too

appealing. I kept saying, 'Bob, they're called *mutant* toys. Make me some toys that'll scare me.'" Bill Cone, fresh from Tim Burton's *Nightmare Before Christmas*, came on board and, along with Ralph Eggleston, helped change the direction with some bizarre suggestions. "Ralph's is the really sick stuff," Lasseter declares, and these preliminary ideas soon got everyone tuned to the same twisted wavelength.

Working in constant consultation with the story team, the art department began piecing together absurdly juxtaposed bodies. "It was a

real back-and-forth process," says Eggleston. "Sometimes the story department tried to find spots for things we dreamed up, sometimes they came to us first with stick figures and said, we need a character to do a particular thing. Joss Whedon had written this one line they just thought sounded funny, 'wind the frog.' So we created a windup frog so Tom Hanks could say that line."

The beauty of the mutant characters is how well they serve story points, as well as boasting sheer graphic impact. The story staff had designed each mutant toy with some

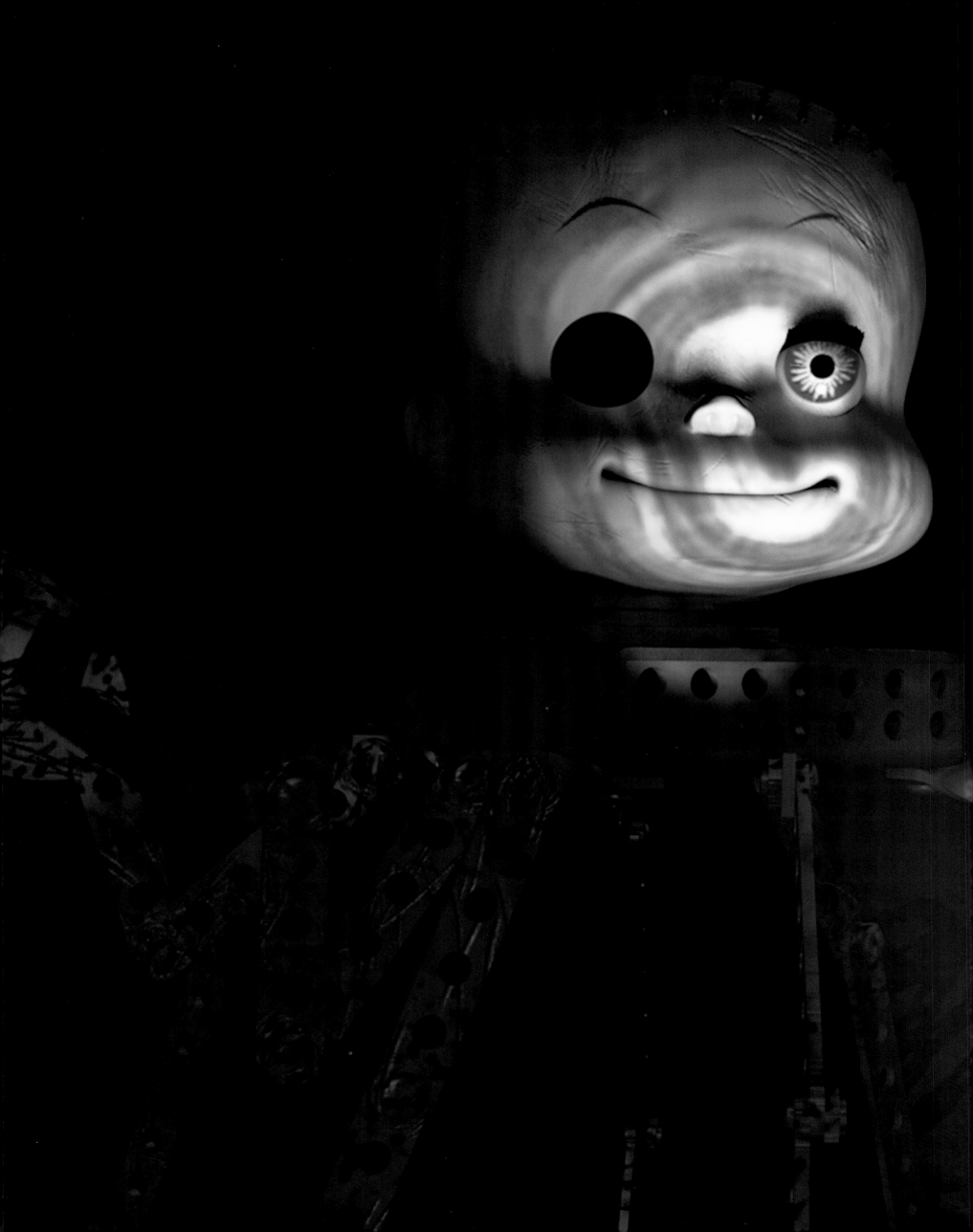

CONCEPT ART BY BILL CONE.

"With the mutant toys, we cobbled them
together from other pieces that they'd modeled
almost the way Sid would have made them,
and then we made shaders to make them look
all dirty and beat up and scratched. And the
animators were inspired because they were
free to come up with very different forms of
motion for these characters."

—RALPH EGGLESTON

CONCEPT ART BY BOB PAULEY.

crucial task in mind that only that toy could perform in the gulag-escape finale. "RollerBob," a soldier doll's upper half screwed to a skateboard, thus became a "jet pilot complete with sun visor and crash helmet," says Lasseter, and flies the escapees down the stairs and out into the backyard. "Legs" uses her shapely, high-heeled gams to steady the fishing rod that rescues "Frog," whose roadster-style wheels make him fast enough to lure away Scud, and so on.

Part of the mutants' startling fluidity stems from the fact that they were among

the last cast members to be modeled and animated. "We had better software tools by the end of production than we had at the start, when we built our main characters," says Eben Ostby. "That's how fast the technology is changing."

In many cases, Eggleston and company raided the modelers' inventory of existing body parts to help speed along the production schedule. Among the familiar components in the mutant lineup: wrestler Rocky Gibraltar's torso is part of the "bug driver" mutant. The skateboard from Andy's room that Buzz uses in

repairing his "ship" is the mobile base for RollerBob. The corpselike hand of the Jack-in-the-box is Woody's own, blown up bigger and bedecked with longer fingernails, stitches, warts, and ugly green paint. But Eggleston is proudest of what the modelers did with the head of Molly, Andy's little sister. "She's reborn as Babyhead. The technical staff just squished her head's x and y coordinates, took an eye out, took the hair off, and put little holes in the head, sewed up the mouth, made the skin plastic, stuck it on an erector set, and there you go."

Above: CONCEPT ART BY BILL CONE.
Center left: CONCEPT ART BY BUD LUCKEY.

"The mutants are selfless in a way that Andy's toys are not. In Andy's room, where everything is so rosy with clouds on the wallpaper, the toys have lots of little peeves with each other. Maybe that just reflects a basic need in people's lives to always have conflict, and so in cushier situations, they find something to disagree about. Nobody needs that in Sid's room, because they've got Sid. It's really about survival there. In a war zone, everybody bands together."

—RALPH GUGGENHEIM

Above: CONCEPT ART BY BOB PAULEY.
Left: CONCEPT ART BY DAVE GORDON.

The Lady and the Hamm

CONCEPT ART BY JEAN GILMORE.

"Our Bo Peep isn't as dainty as you'd expect her to be from her looks. She's more of a city chick than a farm girl."

—GALYN SUSMAN, Lighting Lead

CONCEPT ART BY BUD LUCKEY.

She's a petticoated lady. He's a naked swine. She's made of delicate porcelain, practically fine china. He's crudely porcine, made of a tough, coarse plastic resembling cheap ceramic.

But if you peeled back the computer graphic exteriors of Bo Peep (Annie Potts) and Hamm (John Ratzenberger), you'd find two character models whose base surfaces look identical. It's only when two separate, diametrically different "shader" programs are laid over their smooth, machine-perfect "default" skins that the pink pair become such a study in contrast.

"They're basically at the two extremes of how shaders can depict light hitting a surface," says Eben Ostby, who wrote the computer-code shader for Hamm. "You can make surfaces look very reflective, where you see actual images of surrounding objects bounced back at you, or merely specular, which means

they're kind of dull by comparison and they only reflect plain, white, dotlike highlights from strong light sources."

Hamm, being a bit of a dullard, occupies the nonreflective, purely specular end of the spectrum. "I thought of his surface as the sort of stuff you see in card store gift items, with that unfired-clay look," says Ostby. "He's extremely basic in design in every way." The solid pink plastic-cum-plaster he's made of is decorated by only a few swatches of paint inside his nostrils and ears and two blush circles on his cheeks. Hamm is heavy, which gives him only limited mobility—a trait conveyed not only by the shader's surface information but by the way he's animated. "There's no play in him when he walks," notes Ostby. "He's got these pudgy, stiff legs, no grace to them, which is of a piece with the unexamined life he leads. Bo, on the other hand, has these slender, free arms. She's got a lot of frilly details in the cloth in her dress and her bodice. She's more evolved."

At least, that's how she finally appeared in the movie. Initially, Bo's snow-white skin was going to carry a matte shader finish similar to Hamm's. But that made her look too much like the other plastic doll toys, and left her lost in

crowd scenes. Instead, her skin was pushed up to maximum shininess, then given a series of intricate reflections with a technical trick called a "trace cube." Scores of these cubes, also called "mapped environments," were created to give every polished surface in *Toy Story* a refractive sheen, from Buzz's helmet to the wood floors in Andy's house to the spoon that Woody brandishes like a mirror after Sid burns a hole in his head. Derived by a computer program, they're "like an unfolded cardboard box," says Tom Porter. "The box's six sides represent the four walls, the ceiling, and the floor at whatever spot the character is standing in for that one shot." Automated calculations derived the flattened-out trace cube panels from three-dimensional modeled environments, and then wrapped that flat visual information around the curves of whatever surface needed to carry the reflections.

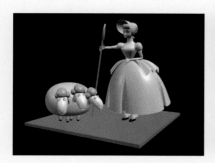 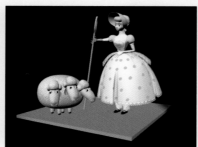  

Left and right: IMAGES OF BO PEEP AND HAMM BEFORE AND AFTER THEIR CUSTOM-DESIGNED SHADER PROGRAMS ARE APPLIED.

In Bo's case, though, a little trace cube technology went a long way. "If we tried to reflect the whole room in her, it got too complicated," says Galyn Susman, who worked on Bo's shader as well as one for her sheep. "Every time she turned her head, she had all this distracting stuff moving over her face. It made her look metallic. So we simplified it." If you examine Bo closely during her scenes with Woody, you'll see that the only objects you can clearly make out in her dazzling surface are Andy's bedroom windows; Woody doesn't show up at all. Of course, that selective, self-possessed exterior truly befits the sort of "woman" Bo is: She's her own shepherdess, not some beautiful reflection of a shy cowboy's interest in her.

Above: TRACE CUBE TECHNOLOGY ALLOWS REFLECTIONS TO BE MAPPED ONTO ANY SURFACE AS SHOWN HERE IN BUZZ'S HELMET AND A SPOON.
Below: A TRACE CUBE OR "MAPPED ENVIRONMENT" OF ANDY'S ROOM TO BE APPLIED TO BUZZ'S HELMET.

CONCEPT ART BY RALPH EGGLESTON.

CONCEPT ART BY TIA KRATTER.

87

> "If these human characters appear to be of their
> world, then we succeeded."
>
> —BILL REEVES

Of all the technical challenges involved in the production of *Toy Story*, none was greater than creating believable human characters. Because of the organic qualities of hair, skin, and clothing—the basic elements of human surface appearance—human characters are among the most difficult objects to make convincing using computer-generated images.

STORYBOARD ART BY ANDREW STANTON.

> "The best thing I learned about engineers is, if
> you say ok you can't do it, they'll kill themselves
> to prove you wrong. It's a challenge for them."
>
> —ANDREW STANTON

"For the humans, I didn't want to attempt super–realism, because we'd fail. I didn't want to make them overly simplified, because they'd wind up looking too much like the toys. The approach had to fall somewhere between cartoonish and real."

—JOHN LASSETER

Above: CONCEPT ART OF ANDY'S LITTLE SISTER MOLLY BY DAN HASKETT.
Right: CONCEPT ART OF ANDY BY BUD LUCKEY.

CONCEPT ART OF ANDY'S MOM BY DAN HASKETT.

When Walt Disney made *Snow White and the Seven Dwarfs* in 1937, the challenge of animating four realistic human characters pushed the staff beyond what anyone had yet done in the medium. A touch as apparently simple as adding a blush to Snow White's cheeks, for instance, required that real rouge be hand-applied to each finished animation cel in exactly the same spot.

For the *Toy Story* staff, creating human characters who seem truly alive presented a similar challenge. "Nobody has ever done a single adequate human in computer graphics," says Tom Porter. "We had to do four. Andy, his mom, Sid, and Hannah all had to look convincing and distinct. That's a very tall order."

"Bar none, humans were the biggest challenge of the entire production," says John Lasseter. Because they knew they would

have better computer tools at their disposal the longer they waited, the modeling, animating, and texture mapping of the human cast was deliberately saved for last in the production pipeline.

An overriding imperative was creating human skin that would be clearly distinguished in color, texture, and movement from the toys' plastic countenances. That challenge sent Porter off into a whirl of biomedical research to amass a grasp of his subject worthy of a dermatologist.

Porter instructed Tia Kratter on exactly what visual information should go into each of ten layers of textural details, including dermal and epidermal skin, fine facial hairs, primary and secondary wrinkles, oil, and blood layers. He then wrote a "shader" program that could instruct rendering software to process thousands of different possible lighting situations

THE FIRST HUMAN CHARACTER PIXAR ATTEMPTED WAS THE BABY CREATED FOR THE SHORT FILM *TIN TOY*.

by sandwiching—in different ratios and at varying degrees of opacity and translucence—those ten layers.

As complex as the skin proved to be, it was child's play compared to the obstacles that clothing presented. The jeans and T-shirt that Sid wears, for instance—probably a simple $50 wardrobe tab in a live-action movie—required an intensive program of

"We're nowhere near substituting virtual actors for real ones. We will never be able to compete with Hollywood's great actors and great faces. What we hope we'll be able to do better and better is create characters who seem real, but who can do things no actor could."

—BILL REEVES

experimentation. Visual minutiae familiar from everyday life, like the precise sort of crinkle jeans make around the knees, called for laborious study and superhuman work schedules. Whole photo albums full of Pixar staffers modeling their faded denims—standing in jeans, sitting in jeans, touching toes in jeans—lined the shelves of Damir Frkovic's office. His onscreen diagrams depicting Sid's pants soon pulsed with more intricate networks of lines than a flight controller's radar screen. "I'm not even that technical a person,"

he insists. "I tailor the shape and the drapery of the clothes. Someone else with more programming skill has to go in and give them all the levers and controls for the animators."

Clever camera angles, the use of close-ups wherever possible, and artful cutting between silhouettes, off-camera voices, and implied actions all helped the artifice succeed. But editorial sleight of hand couldn't be counted on to cover a multitude of technical challenges, from the look of footprints on grass and rugs to the shifts of a shirt sleeve on an

arm. The constant innovation required of the technical team often made them feel more like think-tank scientists than part of a filmmaking crew. "There's no question, when we decided to tackle humans for this movie, we made a difficult commitment," says Porter. "We had to establish a cutting edge that did not exist when we began. In five years, we'll probably have solved a lot of the limitations well enough to build a whole film around humans. But right now, we're still feeling our way along an unknown path."

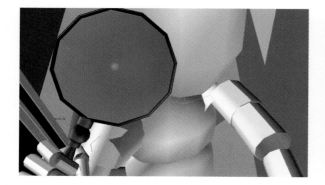

ALL CHARACTERS WERE MODELED AND ANIMATED BY THE SAME PROCESS, BUT THE COMPLEXITY OF THE HUMANS,
AS SHOWN BY THE WIREFRAME AT RIGHT, PROVIDED THE ULTIMATE TEST FOR THE ARTISTS.

CONCEPT ART OF SID'S LITTLE SISTER HANNAH IN HER ROOM BY STEVE JOHNSON.

Above: CONCEPT ART OF HANNAH BY DAN HASKETT.
Right: CONCEPT ART OF HANNAH BY BUD LUCKEY.

"Computers still deal best with stiff, shiny objects. They can make those look utterly real. But as soon as you attempt natural fiber, that's a quantum leap in visual complexity. The softer it is, the tougher it is to model and animate and give it a texture."

—JOHN LASSETER

AN EMOTIONAL JOURNEY

I t wasn't enough to create a world that looked real and populate it with believable-looking characters which moved realistically and told a cohesive story. The one element of storytelling that would be absolutely essential to making *Toy Story* work was emotional believability. Through the use of music, careful voice casting, attention to ambient sound, and subtle work with characters, acting, and lighting, the filmmakers worked to bring a richness and realism to the film that was yet unmatched in computer animation.

STORYBOARD ART BY BUD LUCKEY.

STORYBOARD ART BY BUD LUCKEY.

> "Randy's music really nailed the emotional themes
> for our movie in a way that only music can do."
>
> —BONNIE ARNOLD

As characters and story line came into focus, the filmmakers concentrated on what kind of music might enhance the story. The question of whether to have songs, either sung by characters or played over the score, came up early in development. After much consideration it was ultimately decided that a "song-over-action" score in which a third-person narrator sang about what's happening onscreen was the best approach. The choice of who should execute this music was clear to everyone involved from the first. Randy Newman—composer of such sweeping, Oscar®-nominated film scores as *Avalon*, *The Natural*, *The Paper*, and *Ragtime*—was a natural to find the ideal combination of emotion and irony.

Above and bottom right: STORYBOARD ART
BY ROBERT LENCE.
Top right: STORYBOARD ART BY BUD LUCKEY.

> "The songs became the one place Woody and Buzz really manifest their feelings explicitly. It's
> where they voice stuff they don't otherwise admit to people, or even to each other."
>
> —RANDY NEWMAN, Composer

STORYBOARD ART BY BUD LUCKEY.

> "Randy turned out to be a great help to us when we needed a lot of emotion told to the audience, and accepted by the audience, in a very short amount of time. 'You've Got a Friend in Me' speaks volumes about the love between Andy and Woody, better than we could ever tell it in dialogue. The way you feel at the end of that song, we would have needed two more sequences without a song to get that point across."
>
> —ANDREW STANTON

> "The one great thing a composer can do in animation is he can lead us as much as respond to us. We have a story laid out and we may have a sense of where that song should go, but we looked to Randy to show us through his viewpoint how these characters could move us."
>
> —CHRIS MONTAN

STORYBOARD ART BY JASON KATZ.

Randy Newman's honest emotional reaction when Chris Montan first approached him about writing the music for *Toy Story* was one of trepidation.

The seasoned composer's initial concern in taking on *Toy Story* centered on the unique, first-time-ever nature of its high-tech imagery and action-oriented story line. "I couldn't just get a fairy tale, you know?" Newman says. "I kept thinking, why couldn't they have hired me to retell 'The Troll Under the Bridge' or something regular like 'Jack and the Beanstalk?' But no, I've got to get this weird action movie with this 28th-century technology that nobody's ever done before, and nobody knows how to score."

The first song Newman delivered was "You've Got a Friend in Me," which he came in to unveil personally for Lasseter, Guggenheim, Arnold, and Montan at the Burbank studios on March 26, 1993.

Newman had clearly hit on the right lyrical approach within the song-over-action idiom: The songs would be delivered by him on the final soundtrack, but they'd be structured as interior monologues for the characters onscreen, directly conveying Woody's thoughts in some scenes, Buzz's in others.

Newman carefully considered the puzzle of how the score would work to enhance this technologically advanced film. "If the sound were heavily synthetic and computerized, the whole thing would take on a chill," the composer asserts. Newman and director Lasseter hit almost immediately on the answer to the conundrum: A movie that stakes out a new visual frontier should come wrapped in music of the most conventional instrumental colorations. "The orchestrated sound needed to

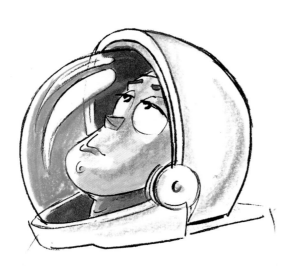

CONCEPT ART BY BUD LUCKEY.

"I have to say there is much more humanity in the finished picture than I anticipated. I don't think I could have ruined the appeal of this thing with six Casios and a nose flute."

—RANDY NEWMAN

STORYBOARD ART BY BUD LUCKEY.

STORYBOARD ART BY JASON KATZ AND BUD LUCKEY.

be laid on very full, because these images soaked a lot of that right up," says Newman.

Newman's songs and arrangements both directly express the characters' thoughts and work as indirect mini-essays on how standard musical styles can cue our feelings. "You've Got a Friend in Me" marries what Newman calls the instrumental timbre of a "New Orleans shuffle" to a western-flavored, clippety-clop underlying rhythm. "It's a comfy, homey sound," says the composer. "Strange Things" is "flat-out rock and roll," a match for Woody's "dazed, hit-in-the-head" state as he watches his most-favored-plaything status

evaporate. The background score, too, ranges freely through a mix of evocative movie music archetypes, from war movie bombast for the soldier's descent on the birthday party to spacey synthesized sound for the weird corridors of Pizza Planet.

The hardest musical sequence to work out, Newman recounts, was "I Will Go Sailing No More." The mood needed to change midway from a mordant, eulogistic lament to a defiant rallying cry as Buzz gets the idea to tempt fate and leap off a railing, and then had to ease back into a mournful mode. "That kind of left turn can easily

make people too conscious of what you're trying to do. You don't want the music to be an alarm clock."

From a slow, gentle wash of strings as Buzz walks dejectedly away from seeing himself in a TV ad, to a soaring, Olympian fanfare as he climbs a banister to jump off and test his wings, to a feathery, descending piano riff as he falls in slow motion, the mood of the final scoring shifts radically, but never breaks. "This," says John Lasseter, "is about as many emotional chords as you can safely hit in one scene. It's the moment when Buzz Lightyear may steal the picture."

Buzz: SHIELD YOUR EYES!
IT'S NOT WORKING. I RECHARGED IT BEFORE I LEFT. IT SHOULD BE GOOD FOR HOURS—
Woody: OH, YOU IDIOT! YOU'RE A TOY!

"Getting a line reading from Tom Hanks is like getting this big, incredibly wet sponge. It's overflowing with different possibilities for you to wring out."

—GLEN McQUEEN, Animator

Vocal tracks are the initial creative spark that inspire the animators to dream up the most expressive gestures possible for their computer-generated characters. The animators match their work to the vocals, not the other way around. The relationship between animator and voice actor is a particularly rich one, since the physical movement together with the voice make up the complete persona of the character onscreen.

STORYBOARD ART BY ANDREW STANTON.

Buzz: OH, I AM A SHAM! I AM A SHAM!   Woody: SNAP OUT OF IT, BUZZ!

Woody: HO HO BOY, AM I GLAD TO SEE YOU GUYS!

CONCEPT ART OF SID'S HOUSE, AS SEEN THROUGH ANDY'S
BEDROOM WINDOW, BY TIA KRATTER.

"There is an unspoken element when you are writing the screenplay and boarding the film, and that is the actors. Once they got involved, they became like a third partner, without actually having to do any work. Because once you know who they are, you know just the attitude to take."

—JOSS WHEDON

Mr. Potato Head: SON OF A BUILDING BLOCK, IT'S WOODY!
Hamm: HE'S IN THE PSYCHO'S BEDROOM!

"We already had the designs for Buzz and Woody done long before Tom
Hanks and Tim Allen were cast, but it's amazing how once we brought the
voices the characters would start to look like Tom and Tim. The models
stay the same but the animators start to adopt their mannerisms."

—BONNIE ARNOLD

Mr. Potato Head: DID YOU ALL TAKE STUPID PILLS THIS MORNING?! HAVE YOU FORGOTTEN WHAT HE DID TO BUZZ?

Holding a rubber prop arm that John Lasseter had given him, Tom Hanks proceeded to mug his way through a string of ad-libs that had his control room audience howling, ranging from excessive back patting to an uproarious faked backrub to a fatuous palm reading to a cuticle manicure to a give-me-five hand slap. Months later, the animation staff was so taken with a videotaped copy of the improvisation session that they meticulously reworked portions of Hanks's routine in animated form, sometimes gesture for gesture.

The animators' greatest guides in working the vocal tracks are simply the inflections the actors have provided. Karen Kiser, who animated several Rex shots, found Wallace Shawn's diction a constant inspiration for the neurotic dinosaur. John Ratzenberger, says John Lasseter, delivered more usable one-liner ad-libs than any other performer. "He was always right in character. His delivery would just be so perfectly smug, you could practically see Hamm lifting his snout up in the air." Tim Allen's "motorcycle cop" demeanor, says Glen

McQueen, always made him think of arched eyebrows and a thrust-out chin for Buzz.

Not that the animators seek simply to replicate or caricature an actor's physical presence. "We try to glean the movements that fit so well and make the voice come alive in movement," says Pete Docter. "The material surrounding one little tic might be completely inappropriate to the character, but you can pick that out and extract it. It's a way to build the perfect take in a way you couldn't if you were making a live-action movie."

Woody: OH, HI BUZZ! WHY DON'T YOU SAY HELLO TO THE GUYS OVER THERE?
"HI YA FELLAS. TO INFINITY AND BEYOND!"

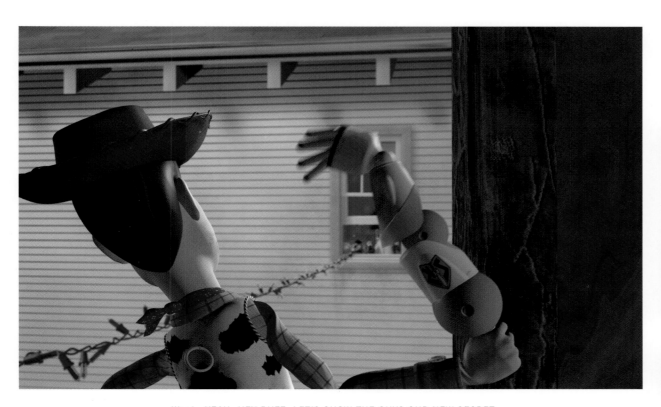

Woody: YEAH, HEY BUZZ. LET'S SHOW THE GUYS OUR NEW SECRET
BEST-FRIENDS HANDSHAKE. GIMME FIVE, MAN!

"We get a lot of ad-libs coming out of the
actors, and I've found that if you keep painting
what the scene is in their mind, that's when
they give you the really great stuff."

—JOHN LASSETER

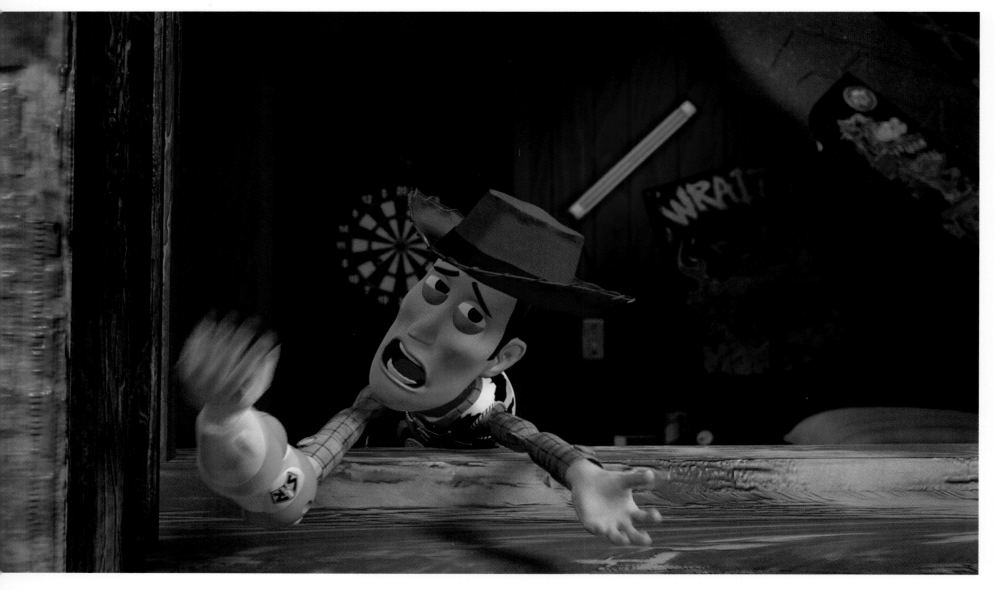

Woody: NO! NO! COME BACK! SLI-I-I-INKYYY!!

STORYBOARD ART BY ROBERT LENCE.

Mr. Potato Head and Slinky

CONCEPT ART BY BUD LUCKEY.

"Potato Head is the spud who would be king."

—RALPH GUGGENHEIM

STORYBOARD ART BY JOE RANFT.

The casting of particular voice talent can be the result of an inspired synchronicity between a character and a known actor. But it is equally likely that the decision to cast an actor to voice a certain role can change the artists' conception of the character. Both models of casting were at work in *Toy Story*.

Ever sarcastic and always ready to think the worst of people, Mr. Potato Head is not the most popular of Andy's playthings. "He'd really like to be in Woody's spot, but Andy doesn't love him as much. That makes him a little jealous," says Ralph Guggenheim. The other toys give him a wide berth, except for Hamm, who probably only befriends him because it makes him feel superior. "Potato's not the brightest guy," says Jason Katz. "If you look at his side of the battleship game with Hamm, he's managed to outline Hamm's ships without hitting any. Then when he loses, he says, 'Are you peeking?' He's always blaming somebody else for his problems."

John Lasseter was determined to cast Don Rickles, stand-up comedy's undisputed king of put-downs, as the resident curmudgeon of Andy's room. The director and Thomas Schumacher made a personal visit to Rickles's home, Mr. Potato Head doll in hand, to pitch the actor on the project. As they presented the toy to Rickles, Lasseter accidentally knocked

CONCEPT ART BY TIA KRATTER.

off the doll's trademark bowler. The sudden, unmistakable resemblance between the bald plastic pate and Rickles's own cracked up everyone present—and broke the ice so well that Rickles quickly agreed to do the part.

While the intrinsically grumpy countenance of Mr. Potato Head quickly inspired the perfect voice casting, the sleepy looks and personality of Slinky, Woody's loyal sidekick, only developed after a long search for an actor to play the character. Slinky was initially designed and modeled as a frisky, nervous puppy—a Jack Russell terrier—with

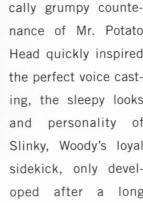

perky ears, a conelike snout, and wide eyes. But early efforts to find a vocal talent that would click with this skittish design, says Ralph Guggenheim, "didn't pan out well at all." Also, alongside neurotic Rex, the eager-to-please Slinky had begun to seem redundant; both characters had a timid, fawning nature.

At a voice casting meeting with Lasseter, Guggenheim, and Bonnie Arnold, Schumacher hit on an inspired answer to the problem. "We

had originally been looking at actors with an ironic edge to them, but then we started thinking, why not go with someone a little different, someone with a rural take to him. And I said, 'What about Jim Varney?'"

Varney wound up striking an ideal note, bringing a low-key, sentimental sound to the character. Says Schumacher, "Varney's rural take on Slinky dovetailed nicely with Woody being a cowboy, and it made sense that this character would be a loyal follower, without being timid like Rex." Unfortunately, the accent didn't fit Slinky's appearance at all, nor did it match the expectations of the animators. So, the modelers rebuilt Slinky's body to fit Varney's down-home Dixie twang. The ears moved from the top of the scalp to the sides of the head, growing longer and floppier. The eyes drooped to half-mast. The neck got a rickety crimp in it, and

CONCEPT ART BY TIA KRATTER.

the skittish, put-upon terrier first pictured in story sketches emerged anew as a droopy, middle-aged, good-ol'-boy bloodhound.

"It took us a while to find Slink's defining trait, which is not that he's a yes man," says Arnold. "It's that he needs somebody to look up to. He's just a happy-go-lucky simpleton, very loyal. And that's why it's so dramatic when he turns against Woody at the window. At that point, even he can't deny that Woody really has done Buzz wrong."

"There are things you can only know about the *Toy Story* characters by listening, and that's a sound man's dream."

—GARY RYDSTROM, Sound Designer

From the earliest script drafts, John Lasseter and sound designer Gary Rydstrom (an Oscar® winner for *Jurassic Park* and *Terminator 2: Judgment Day*) began planning a sonic "ambience" for each *Toy Story* cast member. Each of the sounds was carefully developed to create an individual keynote for the toys and a sense of emotional realism for the entire picture.

"Sound is another enhancement to believability. If the toys have voice boxes blowing words out through a little plastic or porcelain or ceramic mouth, their voices should reflect that."

—JOHN LASSETER

STORYBOARD ART BY JOE RANFT.

"John Lasseter has always worked with the idea that you could get a lot of your story and your characters across with sound," says Gary Rydstrom. *Toy Story* provided the director and veteran sound designer ample opportunity to play with sound as a means to convey emotions and character. With Buzz and Woody, Rydstrom says he had a ball playing with the contrast between their normal-sounding active speaking voices and "the tinnier, prerecorded things they might not be in the mood to say." The vocal processing needs to be kept to a subtle minimum overall, however, because "John didn't go to all the trouble of casting

> "A lot of sounds in *Toy Story* are very nostalgic. The primitive feel is hooking into childlike ideas about toys—what they would be like if they were alive—and memories and fantasies from our own childhoods."
>
> —GARY RYDSTROM

Above: STORYBOARD ART BY JEFF PIDGEON (left) AND JOE RANFT.
Top: CONCEPT ART BY BUD LUCKEY.

these particular voice actors so I could come in and make them unrecognizable."

There was more latitude, says Rydstrom, in the fine-tuned aural essays built around each character's body movements. Bo Peep, for instance, has a delicate, wind-chime air when she moves. "Obviously you're not going to do the sound of moving porcelain, because there's no such thing," Rydstrom explains. "What you can do are the characteristic dinks of porcelain hitting on more porcelain, like if her arm bumps into her staff, and then the little clicks of her feet hitting the ground. You don't need too much of that. It's there to do what the

texture-mapped imaging is doing with her surface. It's reminding you what she's made of."

Although he strove to give *Toy Story* the feel of a real-world, live-action adventure funneled through "low-to-the-ground listening points you're not used to," Rydstrom says that no matter what medium a movie is made in, expressiveness is more important than accuracy. "What's fun about doing this kind of film-making is that you get to base your sound in reality, because these are real toys. At the same time you want to make the sound either have character or have some emotional quality that tells you something about the character."

The peak creative kick for Rydstrom in *Toy Story* was unquestionably the mutant toys, since their "weird combinations gave us the perfect excuse to do something a bit more bizarre." He was delighted by the chance to play on the fears of Buzz and Woody—as well as the audience—as they change their reaction to the mutants' unchanging, trademark whirrings. Says Rydstrom, "The noises they emit don't change at all, but they seem different. By the end of the movie, the way Jingle Joe tinkles makes you feel sorry for him in some ways because it's such a poignant reminder of his predicament."

As the first-ever computer animated feature, *Toy Story* posed a unique challenge to create characters with sustained emotions through 75 minutes onscreen. To make that happen, the animators and technicians worked with precise refinements in the character models and subtle, quiet acting.

STORYBOARD ART BY JILL CULTON.

STORYBOARD ART BY JILL CULTON.

"With each tool you put in for the animators you have to evaluate if it's going to sell the emotion that you want to get out of it. It isn't enough just to give the character anatomy. You've got to give it acting power."

—BILL REEVES

Bill Reeves, who modeled the contours and the keyboard-controlled musculature of Woody's head, tried to put as many human-style muscle controls into the character's face as possible. He found inspiration in sources as diverse as a "visible head" anatomical model kit and a scholarly study of expressions called the "facial action coding system," which analyzes how twenty-five distinct muscle groups in the face combine to reflect various moods. Reeves strove to make Woody not just elaborate but articulate, able to express a full range of complex feelings through the film. In the scene where Woody and Buzz are trapped by Sid, for example, Woody had to project regret, fear, frustration, resignation, and resolve.

Mark Oftedal, who worked on many of the Woody shots in this sequence along with Rich Quade and Pete Docter, found the fineness of Woody's controls indispensable in taking a minimalist approach to the long, sustained close-ups. "It was a chance to do some really subtle, serious acting," he says. Glen McQueen, who along with animator Colin Brady handled many of Buzz's reaction shots, also found that the less choreography he inserted, the better the emotion played. "It's not like the kind of advertising stuff a lot of us are used to, where you have fifteen seconds to capture an entire character and everything's got to be very broad. John kept encouraging us to keep things very small and very quiet." That's a particular challenge in computer

Top right: THE SCULPTURE OF WOODY'S HEAD BY SHELLEY DANIELS.
Bottom right: THE COMPUTER WIREFRAME MODEL.

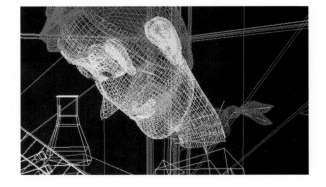

"The eyes, more than anything else, give life to a toy. The angle of a blink, how far the pupils go off to the side when a character is trying to peek at something without being noticed conveys a sense of presence better than any other element."

—JOHN LASSETER

Right and opposite: THE MANY FACES OF WOODY. THE *TOY STORY* ANIMATORS CONCENTRATED ON THE IMPORTANCE OF SUBTLE EYE AND FACIAL MUSCLE MOVEMENTS TO ACHIEVE A CONVINCING EXPRESSION OF THE EMOTIONS OF THE CHARACTERS.

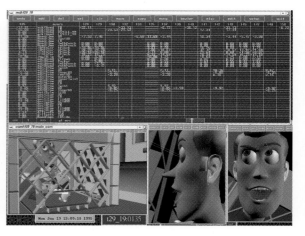

animation because the character you're manipulating can never come to a complete stop, the way it can for emphasis in drawn animation.

Working on the advice of acting coaches who told them that great performances begin and end with the actor's eyes, the filmmakers exploited the technical precision that only computer graphics can provide to capture the precise way we actually use our eyes to scan the visible world. "Your eyes don't glide in a smooth arc when you look at something," explains Ash Brannon. "They dart and lock, dart and lock. It's a jerky motion." In drawn

animation, where lines are coarse, such jittery moves won't work; they look like errors. But the computer-rendered detail in Woody's eyes is so precise in its registration that these little hovering moves look right. "When you watch a character onscreen, you're watching the eyes," says Brannon. "If they're

not alive, then neither is the character."

Another technical advance that accentuates this human quality is a software feature called "eye tracking." It allows the animators to select a point in space for a character to gaze at, and then, unless instructed otherwise, the computer keeps the apparent "eyeline"

"Hold a pose completely still and it jumps out at you immediately as a mistake. The life just dies right out of the character. It might work for a moment of reflection for, say, Wile E. Coyote right before he drops. It won't work for Woody or Buzz pondering their fate. And that forces you to find just that subtle eye flick, or that teeny tilt of a head, that makes them alive."

—GLEN McQUEEN

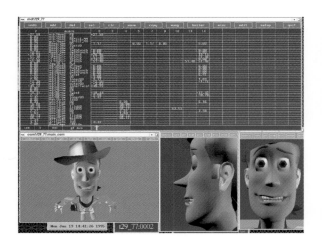

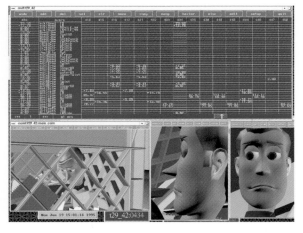

fixed no matter where the head is turned. "It's one more way to lead the audience right to those glances," says John Lasseter.

"There's no better example of the power of eye movement than during the dawn sequence," says the director. "You see Woody's gaze shift to focus on Buzz, and then you can see he's suddenly looking at nothing, really, as he realizes he might die and, maybe worse, that Andy might never play with him again even if he does get back to him. It's all in those tiny, tiny flickers. There's no real question in the audience's mind that these guys have brains and they're mulling all this over."

ART DIRECTOR RALPH EGGLESTON CREATED A PASTEL COLOR SCRIPT FOR THE ENTIRE FILM IN ORDER TO SUGGEST
CHANGES IN COLOR AND LIGHTING THAT WOULD BE INTEGRAL TO SHIFTS IN THE MOOD OF THE STORY.

"Lighting pulls everything together all at once. It's like when you
go by a construction site and see a building that's just a frame. A
few days later you pass it and bam, it's a whole building."

—RALPH GUGGENHEIM

I t was the lighting crew's job to turn scenes of completed animation from unlit shots—which
carry default lighting data that simply delineates objects in the frame without highlighting
any one item—to fully lit environments with a greatly enhanced sense of depth, atmosphere,
and time of day. To determine a lighting strategy for a given scene, the lighting staff relied on a
"color script," created by Ralph Eggleston, which established not only the physical quality of
the lighting but the mood and tone the lighting might evoke in the audience.

"It's extremely time–consuming and complicated to do a slow animation of light sources, but we really wanted to use the lighting in the scene where Woody talks to Buzz when Buzz is tied to a rocket to show how Woody is finally getting through to him, convincing him that he's worth something just for being a toy."

—SHARON CALAHAN, Lighting Lead

They never touched a bulb or plugged in a power cord. They never climbed rigging to hang spotlights or to cover them with different colored gels. But the *Toy Story* lighting team, led by lighting leads Galyn Susman and Sharon Calahan, and supporting lighting leads Lisa Forssell, Bill Wise, Deborah Fowler and Tien Truong, employed the virtual-world equivalent of nearly every type of lighting source that a live-action filmmaking crew might use—including the sun. "Except we can make our sun come out whenever we want it to, and stay at whatever spot in the sky we desire," laughs Susman.

Instead of physical equipment, however, a computerized menu system did the job. If a "solar source" was selected by Susman at her workstation, then the scene she called up onscreen to light was instantly flooded with rays that stayed parallel all through the space, "just the way real sunlight behaves." But the lighting technician can also select "point sources," or simulations of every conceivable type of man-made illumination. Point-source options include key lights to provide primary "light pointers" to single out the character or object most important in the shot; rim lights to bring out the edges of the characters' faces and give them a more rounded aspect; bounce lights to simulate, say, late afternoon sun reflecting up off Andy's desk as Woody tries to knock Buzz behind it; and fill lights to balance out all the other sources aimed at the characters' bodies.

Once a light source was placed relative to the action, its properties could be fine-tuned almost infinitely. Menu slider bars changed the light's color, the color of the shadows it cast, the darkness or brightness of those shadows, the sharpness or fuzziness of the shadow edges, the shape of the light source, even the "rate of falloff," or the rapidity with which its rays fade as they radiate outward. "It's when you're lighting big groups that you call on all these sort of tight, spotlight-style options the most," says Susman. "If you place Rex, who's dark green, next to Bo, who's all whites, you can't use one big light source. If you set the right brightness level for Rex, Bo gets completely bleached out and disappears. Light it for her and he goes so dark he looks like a charred cinder." Because of these

differences, each character in an ensemble shot needed its own little battery of point sources, sometimes up to thirty separate lights in one shot.

Before a single sequence in the movie was lit, Eggleston mapped out an overall progression of dominant hues for the entire film, usually choosing one or two key colors for each scene. Andy's room, for instance, is flooded with sun and "all warm yellows"; the gas station where Buzz and Woody lose Andy is "lit by a blue moon and by green fluorescents above the pumps"; and Sid's morguelike stronghold is predominantly black light, with stark, ghastly highlights provided by a single, unshaded bulb hanging over Sid's desk.

Perhaps the most striking color planning involved Buzz's plunge out of Andy's window. A warm, reddish, late afternoon glow was contrasted with cool blue light from the eastern sky to set up a visual tension and provide the peak flashes of vibrancy in the entire film. "It's very intense and heightened, because this is where the action takes the most important turn," says Eggleston. The scene has its "exact opposite" late in the movie, as Buzz and Woody await execution at Sid's hands.

A TOTAL OF NINE "POINT SOURCE" LIGHTS WERE USED TO LIGHT THE SCENE IN WHICH WOODY KNOCKS BUZZ OUT OF THE WINDOW.
Left to right: SOFT BLUE RIM LIGHT, VIOLET FILL LIGHT, YELLOW RIM LIGHT, ORANGE KEY LIGHT, AND THE FINAL SHOT.

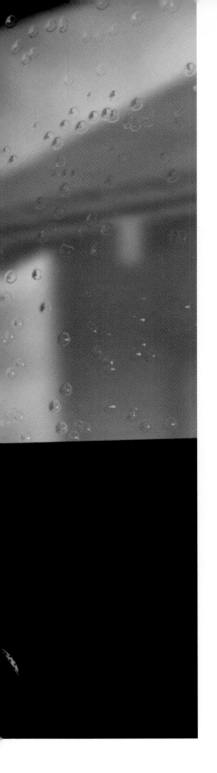

STORYBOARD ART BY JEFF PIDGEON
AND JOE RANFT (bottom).

"Because we're not trying to blend this with either animation or live action, we can let it be its own art form. I think it's going to surprise people what can be achieved using the lighting for mood and tone during a scene. And we're just scratching the surface."

—RALPH GUGGENHEIM

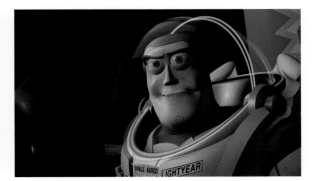

Left to right: AS BUZZ AWAITS HIS EXECUTION THE LEVEL OF THE LIGHT SOURCES ARE ANIMATED SO THAT THE LIGHTING CHANGES AS THE SCENE PROGRESSES, GOING FROM A SOMBER MONOCHROMATIC BLUE TO A WARMER SUNLIT YELLOW.

"The mood there is the lowest point in the story, so we planned the color to start out monochromatic, very blue and cold, almost funereal," explains Eggleston.

"This is the only scene where we actually animated the level of the light sources, slowly bringing them up as the scene progressed," says Sharon Calahan, who handled the entire dark-to-daylight metamorphosis. "At the beginning of the scene, the sun is just barely up and it's behind some heavy rain clouds and the mood is really somber. As soon as Buzz begins to hear Woody and realize that he does have a meaningful life as a toy, the rain stops and it starts to lighten a bit; the color becomes less blue. It doesn't become really bright yet, but there's an easing of the gloomy feel of the scene. And then when Buzz decides to take action the scene brightens dramatically. The sun has broken through the clouds and there's a new day, there's hope."

Rendering

THIS FINAL FRAME OF SID'S DESK REQUIRED TWO HOURS TO RENDER.

Seventy-five minutes of mathematical formulas projected onscreen is what *Toy Story* might look like without the computer technology known as "rendering." Rendering software is the tool whereby mathematical data is recast into a full-color image. "The rendering process is what actualizes the art," says animation scientist Brian Rosen. "It's what we use in place of a pencil on paper, or a brush on canvas, or a chisel on a block of stone."

"There's three basic levels of complexity we use rendering to deliver, each more finished than the last," explains Tom Porter. "How much detail you need depends on what production phase you're in."

The first rendering pass is simply the polygonal rendering displayed on the animators' workstations that gives the animators rough-hewn stand-ins to work with. This stage provides enough building-block visual information to judge the action, but keeps the computers responsive at something close to "real-time" speed.

When the process moves to lighting and shaders, the level of rendering detail is cranked up to about 520 lines of resolution. That is about the resolution of a typical television set and as much as is needed for most color corrections and lighting decisions.

The third and final stage of rendering results in the finished image that appears in the final film. In a single finished frame of *Toy Story*, there are over 1.4 million individual pixels. They're fine enough to form an image that looks so detailed, you'll never see the individual dots, even on a movie theater screen. The resolution of these finished frames is triple that used for the lighting phase, about 1,500 lines.

At this point in the rendering process, jagged edges or unpleasantly hard outlines between objects are removed by "anti-aliasing" routines in Pixar's Renderman software that automatically calculate the pixels to produce the illusion of a smoother finish. "Motion blur," a rendering technique designed to reproduce the blurred effect created when objects move rapidly on film, is calculated for each frame according to how fast an object is moving. There are even rendering calculations to simulate the precise look of lens flare, a distinctive pattern of discs that appears in live-action footage when a bright light shines directly into the camera.

The formidable computational power required to determine the exact tone and hue of each final pixel is controlled through a facility called Pixar's "render farm." The purpose of the facility is to "farm out" frames from each shot to any of the 300 computers that are dedicated to rendering images 24 hours a day.

The average time required to render a final frame is three hours, though some of the most complex could take up to 24 hours to render. "Fast as today's machines are, this is still a slow process," says Porter. Some of the biggest data-eaters include shots involving trees—thanks to all those tiny leaves—and Andy's bedspread. "That was a mighty expensive bedspread," laughs Rosen. "It has some really intricate surface patterns, and has to deform in geometrically complex ways, so the number of calculations involved for each frame is enormous."

Once a shot has been farmed out and rendered, it's the job of the "render wrangler" team to check that the rendering on each frame was correct. One at a time, the frames are examined and approved, then sent off to be filmed. For a 77-minute movie, that means the process had to be repeated over 110,000 times. Without computers to handle the monumental mathematical tasks involved, Pixar's technicians would be unable to finish so much as one shot, let alone an entire movie.

> "No matter what else had to be fixed, we knew where we'd
> eventually be landing. That helped me on mornings when I got up
> saying, what made us think we could make a movie?"
>
> —JOHN LASSETER

To execute a truly emotionally satisfying ending for *Toy Story*, the filmmakers would need to resolve all the plot twists and emotional threads that had been established through the course of Woody and Buzz's journey, while maintaining the principle of believability and adhering to the fundamental internal rules of the basic story. One of the main issues to be resolved, before the protagonists could return home, was how to deal with Sid and with the mutant toys left behind at Sid's house.

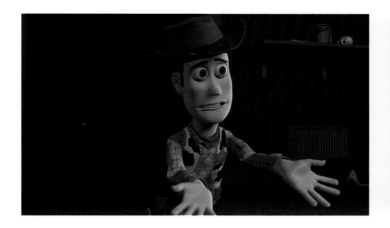

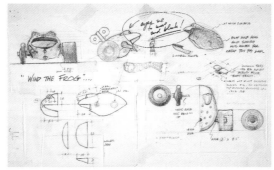

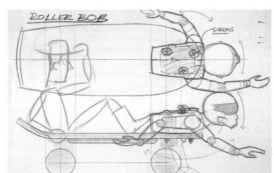

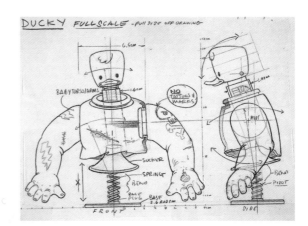

MUTANT TOY MODEL PACKET ART
BY BOB PAULEY.

> "If we left the situation at Sid's house unresolved, it would be like a hostage movie where
> two guys break out but everybody else gets left behind with the terrorists. You wouldn't feel
> very satisfied with that. You sure wouldn't be primed for the chase after the moving van,
> either. We somehow had to leave Sid's house knowing he'd never treat toys badly again."
>
> —ANDREW STANTON

"If you've been playing Dr. Frankenstein but you don't know your creatures are alive, it's definitely going to scare the daylights out of you to find that out."

—JOHN LASSETER

Above: STORYBOARD ART BY BUD LUCKEY.
Right: CONCEPT ART OF SID'S BACKYARD BY RALPH EGGLESTON.
Below: STORYBOARD ART BY BUD LUCKEY AND ROBERT LENCE.

From the earliest script drafts, one inviolable directive was established: Toys must never appear to move or speak under their own power if they think a human might see them. But when it came time to settle the fate of Sid Philips in some dramatically satisfying way, the case for breaking that rule proved too persuasive to resist.

"We got to a point in development where we really faced a bind trying to wrap up a whole bunch of things in that one goodbye-to-Sid scene," says Andrew Stanton. First the audience had to be shown that Sid would somehow change his toy-abusing ways, and not go right on tormenting the mutant toys once

Buzz and Woody escaped. There also had to be a way to make Woody the prime agent of this repentance, a goal that wasn't met in early versions of the story where Woody simply observed while another mutant led the charge against Sid. Says Robert Lence, "That scenario made Woody a supporting character at the very moment he needed to be the star."

As often happens in story development, these seemingly insoluble narrative dilemmas led the staff to reconsider the ground rules they'd set up in the first place, and the unthinkable was proposed: What if Woody bawled Sid out by talking to him directly? "My first reaction was, no way," says Stanton.

Above: CONCEPT ART OF THE SHED IN SID'S BACKYARD BY TIA KRATTER.
Right: STORYBOARD ART BY JOE RANFT AND JILL CULTON (bottom).

"It was very late in the game when we brought all our star mutants down into the backyard. We wanted to show that Woody could really orchestrate them, that he could become a better leader at Sid's house, under adverse circumstances, than he ever was at Andy's."

—JASON KATZ

"But then we realized, why not? As long as we were careful not to break the premise anywhere else, it could work."

It took several additional months before the final stroke fell into place: Woody would speak almost his entire monologue from his scratchy, feeble voice box, moving his lips only for the final few words. "We spent a long time envisioning the scene with Woody just talking plainly to Sid," says Stanton. "It's so much better to have Woody win the day using the one lowly function he's equipped with, the cheap voice box that Potato Head is always making fun of him for, and that he's ashamed of once he hears Buzz's digital chip."

The scene went over much more satisfyingly, too, with the mutant toys from Sid's room rising zombielike from spots all over Sid's yard. Calling out the mutants one more time also allowed the story team to have some fun inflicting on Sid the same mind games he plays on his little sister. "The whole horror movie mood came out of the idea that Sid would be seeing his own creations come alive for the first time," says Katz. "He reacts exactly the way we've already seen Woody and Buzz react. Except by this time, the audience knows the mutants wouldn't hurt anybody. So you get to watch Sid freak out with impunity."

The Chase

For inspiration in staging their kinetic, can-you-top-this computer animated climax, the filmmakers tooled through hours upon hours of the greatest chase scenes in live-action movies. They cut together their own video reel, sampling footage of rubber-burning rides through the choked streets of New York, San Francisco, and L.A.; twisty cat-and-mouse games along deserted cliff drives; and myriad other pursuits set everywhere from southwestern American deserts to Middle Eastern markets. "We wanted to exploit certain ingrained, archetypal elements in that imagery to make our movie seem real," says Edwin Catmull.

To infuse the sequence with the sense of action an audience expects from a "real" movie, restraint was the byword. "A good director only uses a fixed set of lenses to give his film a cohesive look, so that's all we wanted," says Craig Good. "We've only created four or five simulated lenses to 'shoot' our chase locations, even though we could use an infinite variety of focal lengths. In fact, we never used more than that set throughout the whole movie.

"It's a restriction that actually makes computer animation play more realistically, but it's rarely observed," continues Good. "Most animators tend either to use one wide-angle lens and just move the camera forward or back until they've got the framing they want, or to keep the camera the same distance from the action and use dozens of different focal lengths to change the framing from shot to shot. There's no sense of strong, simple visual contrast if you do that, and it certainly doesn't look like standard motion picture imagery."

Keeping the sheer size of movie screens in mind was a deciding aesthetic factor for the chase. "The timing of movement across the frame on a large screen is completely different from what you might do if you have TV in mind," says Good.

The bigger you project a chase scene, the more detail the audience is going to see in the surrounding areas. "It's a whole world," says Ralph Eggleston. "It's not like Andy's room, where the outside only shows in one little window and you can just do a flat background painting of some trees and a little sky and it'll work. Everything had to pass through a recognizable neighborhood, with houses and buildings and intersections on every block. It was pretty scary thinking about constructing all that. We had to build and model almost everything back to the vanishing point for the chase, because it's all visible all the time."

The storyboard shots that showed Buzz and Woody soaring high into the sky were particularly challenging from a technical standpoint. "If the characters are moving forward in space, looking down at the earth, and you're traveling forward with them, that's exceedingly difficult," says Eggleston. "It becomes infinite. You've got to do a whole line of trees, ten or twelve cars, and 125 buildings all the way to the horizon line." The task was a bit easier in shots where the camera would move parallel to the vehicles along the road. Everything immediately behind the action still had to be rendered in depth, but for the farthest away elements, painted backdrops, or flats, could be used instead. "If something is more than a few blocks from the curb, it's not going to change perspective appreciably as you pass it," says Bill Reeves. A painted backdrop, panned slightly and then sandwiched in behind the fully rendered dimensional layer, worked fine. "Side shots are generally much, much easier," says Eggleston. "It's like you're rotating past a turntable, so you can get away not only with flats, but with certain repetitions in the nearby dimensional objects, too."

Since Eggleston did not want anybody to be able to easily spot recurring background motifs, a "stock" group of 14 house lots and 15 building lots were custom colored, positioned, and landscaped into over 125 variations, then set out one next to the other within the largest virtual space "model" in the whole film, stretching scale mile after scale mile.

In one visual respect, *Toy Story*'s chase has a major advantage over a live-action chase: the lighting, the weather, and the time of day are absolutely consistent in every single shot. "In real movies, it can take days to shoot a chase scene," says Ewan Johnson. "You're forced to cut together shots where the sun is directly overhead some of the time, and slanting and creating strong shadows at other times. We don't have any of those problems." The subliminal impact of that consistency, says Johnson, impresses even the jaded eyes of veteran computer-graphics artists. "It's a truly contiguous chase, in real time. That has never been seen before. It's a subtle thing. But if you're a real film buff, or you're a cinematographer, that subtle thing is so convincing, it's disorienting. Your brain keeps saying, it can't be real, it's real, it can't be real."

STORYBOARD ART BY JOE RANFT AND (first row center) ANDREW STANTON.

Above: CONCEPT ART BY JEFF PIDGEON.
Right: CONCEPT ART BY BUD LUCKEY.

"We learned as we worked on the ending that we couldn't just end with a chase. We had to resolve every one of our narrative threads while handling the action. If we didn't have a whole group of satisfying character moments in there, the chase would mean nothing."

—JOHN LASSETER

Though it's dizzying as a technical showcase, Woody and Buzz's odyssey wouldn't amount to much more than a cheap-thrill roller-coaster ride if it weren't for the sense of resolution that grounds it in more lasting ways. In the four long years it took to make *Toy Story*, the prospect of the chase scene's satisfying payoffs—Buzz demonstrating true heroism and physical courage, and Woody, now humbly unconcerned with whether Andy loves him most, at last reunited with the boy— sustained the filmmakers through seemingly endless technical hurdles and story snags.

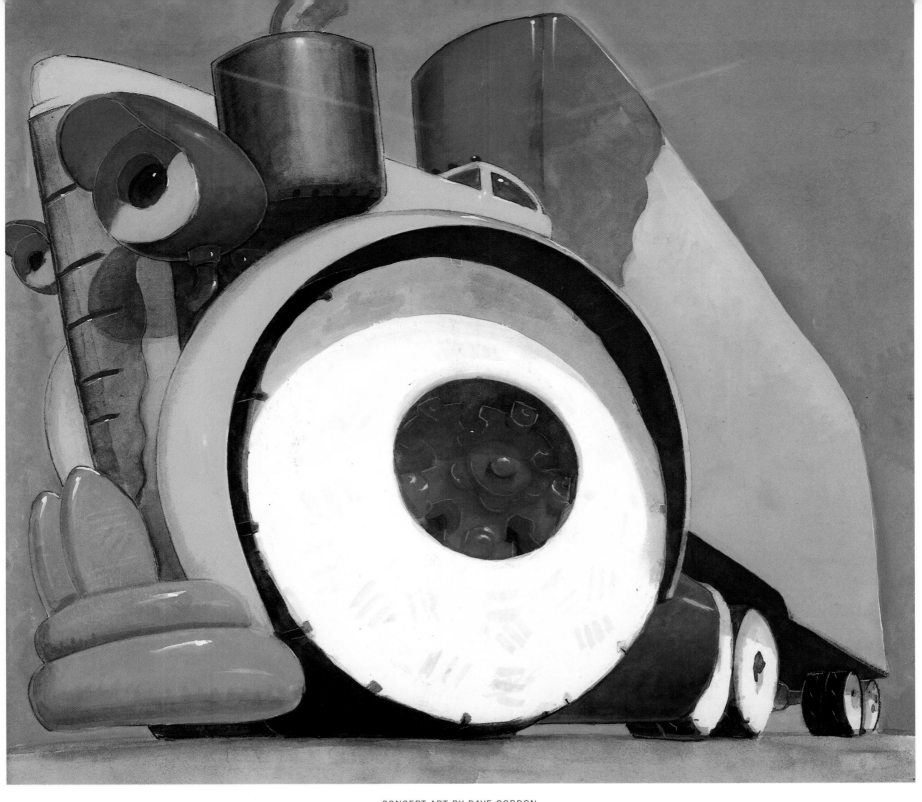

CONCEPT ART BY DAVE GORDON.

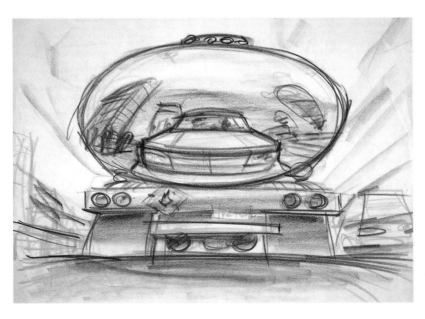

Above and right: CONCEPT ART BY BOB PAULEY.

"Imagine you're riding on the hood of a car doing 90, chasing a ten-story building."
—CRAIG GOOD

CONCEPT ART BY BOB PAULEY.

STORYBOARD ART BY BUD LUCKEY.

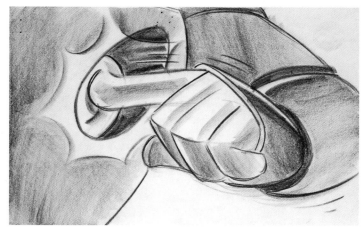

STORYBOARD ART BY BUD LUCKEY.

"Of all the ideas in the movie, only two things never, ever changed. We always had the idea that our main characters were going to get lost in the outside world, and we always pictured them getting back to Andy with a big long chase. We boarded all the moving van stunts early on and they stuck. Thank God we had that ending, or I don't know if we'd have made it."

—JOHN LASSETER

STORYBOARD ART BY JILL CULTON.

Left to right: STORYBOARD ART BY BUD LUCKEY, JEFF PIDGEON, AND JOE RANFT.

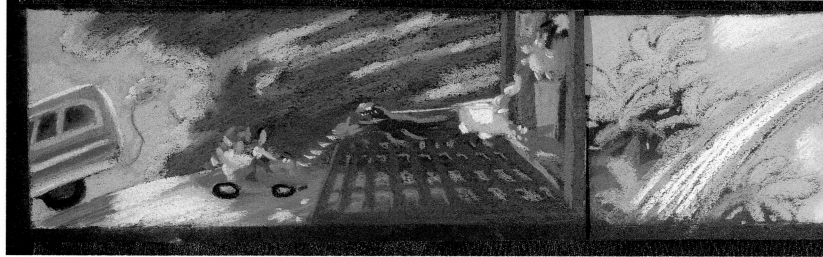

CHASE SEQUENCE COLOR SCRIPT BY RALPH EGGLESTON.

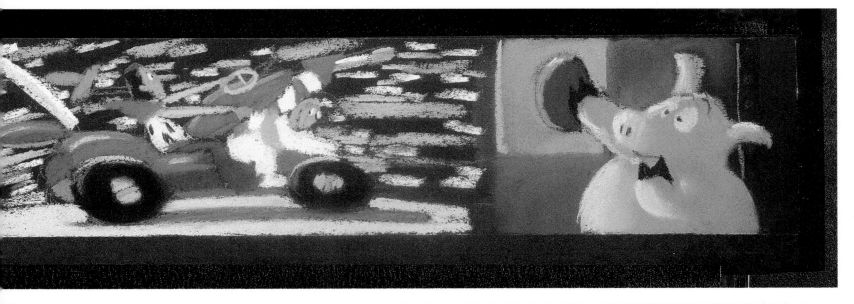

STORYBOARD ART BY BUD LUCKEY.

With the release of *Toy Story* another page in the history of feature-length animation has turned. Like the creators of *Snow White and the Seven Dwarfs* fifty-eight years before them, the makers of *Toy Story* have blazed a trail, introducing a brand new medium in animation.

Those legendary first-ever animation filmmakers could not have known before they began whether their film would be able to hold the minds and, even more, the hearts of their audience. The *Toy Story* creators faced a similarly daunting unknown: Would audiences sit through a full-length animated film and watch computer-generated characters and sets? Would the story hold their attention? Would the film be interesting, funny, emotionally satisfying? Most important—would this relatively unexplored medium be compelling enough to sustain a full-length feature film?

With respect to technical sophistication, it is ironic to think that in the very near future *Toy Story* may well look like the worst of its kind. Such an observation points to the rapid growth of the computer medium and the greater and greater proficiency of the artists who use it. But to speak of technology alone is to focus only on the instrument.

The real secret of what makes *Toy Story* live lies in the strength of its story, the artistry of the animators, and the warmth, humor, and sensitivity of each of the artists and technicians who made their mark upon this film.

The medium is only the vehicle. In the end, *Toy Story* is a film that comes from the heart.

—EDITOR